I Love You Too Much

ALICIA DRAKE is a writer. She was educated at
Cambridge University, and she recently returned to the
United Kingdom after residing and working in Paris
for the past eighteen years. *I Love You Too Much*
is her first novel.

Also by Alicia Drake

The Beautiful Fall

'Funny, waspish, astute, *I Love You Too Much* is a heartbreaking tale.' DENISE MINA, author of *The Long Drop*

'There's an elegance to Drake's writing that marks her out as a writer to be reckoned with and she shows fearlessness as she explores the mind of that most troublesome of creatures, the teenage boy . . . a considerable achievement' JOHN BOYNE, *Irish Times*

'Drake nails the plight of a protagonist caught between childhood and the alarming onset of adulthood, but also elicits a pang of sympathy for Paul's shambolic parents, bruised by their own upbringings . . . a very enjoyable first novel.' *Daily Mail*

'Drake's characters are richly drawn in a coming-of-age novel replete with evocations of adolescent loneliness and insecurity.' *Observer*

'There is the most extraordinary sensibility in this book. It is the author's but she gives it to the reader as thirteen-year-old Paul's out of kilter, isolated, yearning perception. Denied love, this vulnerable boy floats, adrift, through Paris like a lost, living ghost. We see – and feel – through his eyes, and the experience is unsettling, unnerving, strangely delicious. Alicia Drake has achieved something very rare.' TIM PEARS, author of *The Horseman*

ALICIA DRAKE

I Love You Too Much

PICADOR

First published 2018 by Picador

This paperback edition first published 2018 by Picador
an imprint of Pan Macmillan
20 New Wharf Road, London N1 9RR
Associated companies throughout the world
www.panmacmillan.com

ISBN 978-1-5098-4893-5

1 3 5 7 9 8 6 4 2

A CIP catalogue record for this book is available from the British Library.

Printed and bound by CPI Group (UK) Ltd, Croydon, CR0 4YY

I Love You Too Much

Everyone thinks they know Paris: the Eiffel Tower and the old man playing an accordion in the street, couples kissing in cafes and horse-chestnut blossom on fire in the green trees.

They don't know about the secret code to get into your apartment building. They don't know about waiting for the lift to come, watching the thick black cable churn up the lift shaft. They've never been to a children's party here, never felt the party entertainer grab their wrist and say between his teeth: 'That is enough.' *Ça suffit.*

There are no dirty shoes in the 6ème where I live. There is nowhere to get dirty. There are only pavements and the Jardin du Luxembourg. There is grass in the jardin, but you are not allowed to walk on it. And when there is snow they close the jardin, and when there is wind they put up a sign that says danger: risk of violent winds, beware of falling branches.

My Paris is the one same street between school and home. It is grey apartment buildings and heavy wooden doors that you step through into dark courtyards, still and damp where the ivy grows. My Paris is the sound of the concierge's hoover banging up against the front door and water pipes flushing baths away above my head. It is empty corridors of polished parquet four floors up and my feet not touching the ground. I hear the neighbours shout when Paris Saint-Germain score. I hear the surge of the rubbish truck at night in the street below. It is many lives lived alone.

I was a child once in Paris.

1

It was September, the sky was big and blue and Paris felt new again. I stood alone with my back against the wall. Warm drafts of stale air puffed at my legs from the vents in the concrete. There were grey circles on the ground all around my feet, chewing gum spat out and left for dead.

The other kids were pushing to get to the metal barriers that stopped us from spilling out into the road: girls and boys kissing hard, lighting up, texting, swearing at each other. They gathered like flies on a wall. There were girls screaming in tight jeans; they had breasts that showed and mouths that promised. The boys sat astride their mopeds and checked their phones; they reached down to pluck up the shiny club flyers that lay in a pool on the pavement. No one wanted to go home. No one wanted to be alone.

I looked up and saw him waiting. He was chatting on his phone, laughing behind his gold aviator sunglasses. He had a beard to match his brown leather jacket. He had let the beard grow when we were in Saint-Tropez that summer. He was sitting in my mother's car with the music pumping so that I could hear it from where I stood.

He looked up and saw me watching.

'Hey, mate,' he shouted from across the street.

I was not his mate.

'Paul,' he shouted again, 'let's go.'

I waited for a van to go past and then I crossed the street to the car.

'What are you doing here?' I asked.

'Get in and I'll tell you.'

He turned the key in the ignition as I slammed the door shut.

'So you wanna know the news?' he said. His teeth were aimed straight at me.

I shrugged.

'Sure you do, Paul. You can't help yourself.'

I looked away across the street. A guy from school was riding his moped along the pavement through the crowds. A girl sat behind him; she threw back her head and laughed as he weaved in and out of the scared-looking kids. Her long hair flew about her face so that all I could see was her open mouth.

'I'm a dad, Paul. Can you believe that? I'm a dad and that makes you a big brother. Wait until you see her, she's too beautiful.'

'Have you got anything to eat?' I said.

'Is that all you can say?'

She's not my sister, I wanted to say, but it was too late for that.

He swerved out onto the road. There was the sound of brakes and a car hooted behind us.

I saw him check himself out in the rear-view mirror.

'Where are we going?' I said.

'To the hospital.'

'I'm hungry.'

'We'll pick something up on the way.'

We passed the queue outside the bakery: kids, nannies, babysitters from Estonia, older kids from school all lined up outside. That's where I go for sandwiches at lunch, if I'm not having noodles from the noodle bar. I like watching the blue flames leap up around the noodle pan and I like the sweet peanut sauce. If we have time Pierre and I cross the Jardin du Luxembourg to go to McDo's on the Boulevard Saint-Michel. We take the boxes back into the jardin and we sit on the metal chairs and watch the couples kissing wetly under the trees as we suck the red sauce off our chicken nuggets.

Maman doesn't let Cindy buy our bread here; she says it is not artisan. She makes Cindy buy the bread at Kayser, where the baguette has seeds all over that get stuck in my brace and maman says it is good for me. But I like the bread here. I like bread with white flesh that I can roll into moist balls between my fingers and a crust that breaks into tiny shards that prick my skin.

I like their pépites de chocolat too, if I get to the baker in the afternoon at 15.50, which I can do after maths on a Tuesday, then they are just coming out of the oven. They are soft and long and warm. The woman behind the counter wraps them in a small thin sheet of paper that is like tracing paper, white with pale blue lettering. They droop in my hand. The chocolate chips inside are warm and smeary; the dough moulds to the roof of my mouth, and the chocolate turns to liquid under my tongue.

5

I wished it were Cindy picking me up. When Cindy comes, she takes me to the bakery and she buys me two pépites de chocolat and a bag of cats' tongues, flat, green acidy bands covered in granules of hard white sugar that scrape the tip of my tongue. She buys them with her own money so that maman won't find out because maman doesn't want me eating that stuff.

But Cindy was probably at home, standing in the shower with her flip-flops on, spraying down the surfaces and the shower floor with Mr Clean, picking at the dirt between the tiles with a kitchen knife. And Gabriel had come instead.

He rested one hand on the steering wheel and with the other he reached into his leather jacket and pulled out a cigar. He lit it at the traffic lights by the Hôtel Lutetia. He sucked at it so that it burned red. 'Too bad you don't smoke,' he said, looking across at me. He had the seat heating on and it was burning like a furnace beneath me.

'Can't you turn the heating off?' I asked.

'Don't you like a hot arse, Paul?' He smiled at me and revved the engine so that the woman in the car next to us turned and stared. I remembered his hand on my mother's arse, stroking her butt as she lay out beside the pool in Saint-Tropez. She was bursting out of her bikini with her breasts heavy from pregnancy and his hand on her arse, and she never told him to stop. He looked back at the road. 'One day you will,' he said and he laughed out loud.

We were on the Boulevard Raspail, near where my dad

lives. I sent a text to my dad. 'On my way to the hospital,' I wrote, 'to see the baby.' He must have seen the text. He spends his life on the phone: client-watching, emails, calls. But he didn't reply.

'Kind of typical that your mother chooses the most expensive hospital in Paris to have her baby,' Gabriel said; his beard was flecked with gold and he was still tanned from the summer. He had a strand of dark tobacco caught on the unshaven hair above the pink of his upper lip.

'You gotta love that,' he said.

'Neuilly isn't Paris,' I said and I turned away to look at the buildings as we drove west along the quai past the Musée d'Orsay and Les Invalides. We went there in my last year of junior school. We saw Napoléon's horse. It doesn't look like a horse; it looks like a greyhound. It is fine-boned with a coat of thin beige suede. They've stuffed it and put it in a glass case. I don't know how it carried Napoléon. I don't know how it didn't just split right down the middle when he got on it to cross the Alps.

The Seine ran beside us, silvery and magnetic in the late afternoon sun. A barge went by, sliding low through the water, loaded up with black gravel, getting out of Paris. 'Freedom' it said on the side of the barge. There was a white Renault Mégane parked up on deck. It must be nice to go somewhere, to escape.

The funny thing is, I used to want a baby brother, I used to want one so badly, but she always said she didn't want another baby.

'It's you, my baby,' maman used to say when I was six,

7

when everyone else's mothers were having them. She kept her pills in her handbag, a foil packet with pills going round the outside and the days of the week abbreviated on the back in a loop. I used to hope that she would forget her pill, that she would leave the peach-coloured pill in the Sunday socket and that by Monday a baby would be growing, hanging from inside her, like a grape.

And then she went and got pregnant when I was in senior school, when everyone else's mother had stopped doing that. And she did it with Gabriel. She said she didn't know how it happened. I heard her telling Estelle it would be madness to keep it, that Gabriel was four years younger than her, that she hardly knew him, they'd been together only four months. She said he had no money, that he lived in the back end of the 10ème arrondissement and he played guitar in some unknown band.

'He says it's just a question of time before they make it big,' she told Estelle. 'But, I mean, if he's undiscovered at age thirty-five, it's not happening.'

She was in the salon on the telephone when she said that, standing in front of the mirror that hangs above the fireplace, turning to watch the shape her body made. 'But at the same time it could be cute, you know?' She stroked her taut stomach. 'Having a baby. This could be my last chance. And what if it's a girl? I've always wanted a little girl.'

The car jerked to a stop at the lights. I looked across at Gabriel and he must have thought I wanted to speak to him because he started talking again.

'You know, Paul, I didn't think it would be like this. It's big, you know, a big feeling.' He laughed, a strange, anxious laugh. 'And I wonder if I can do it. I mean, am I up to being a dad? I've never done it before.' His phone rang. 'I cried when the doctor pulled her out. Can you believe that, Paul?'

He answered the phone and his voice changed to his French-lover voice, like he was in a film.

'Yes, my love, how is that beautiful little girl of mine? Tell her daddy is on his way.' My mother said something and when he spoke again it was in his normal voice. 'Yeah, yeah, don't stress, babe, we are on our way. I've got the bag. I've got everything. Paul? Yeah, I've got him. We're on the Champs, we'll be there in ten minutes.'

Gabriel took a right turn off the Champs-Élysées, dipping down into the underpass. The last time I was in this tunnel my parents and I were on our way to my grandparents for lunch. My dad was driving. We were late and my parents were arguing. I was in the back gaming, trying to block them out. The smell of maman's scent lay heavy on the leather seats. She was putting on her lip-gloss, making her mouth sticky and round.

'Have you got the macaroons, Séverine?' my dad had asked.

'No,' maman said. She pressed her lips together and smiled at herself in the mirror.

'Where are they?' he said.

She snapped the sunshade back up. 'No idea.'

He held the steering wheel tight.

'You do this on purpose, you do it to piss me off, to upset my mother, I know you do.'

'You're right,' she said, turning to stare at him. 'I do.'

'You're a bitch, Séverine,' he said.

'Perhaps.' I saw her shrug her shoulders as she said that and she looked away out of the window at the grey tunnel wall. 'But it's you that made me that way.'

It used to be hot, molten anger between them that ended in kissing, their bodies thrust up against each other. I was used to that. But this was a new anger; it was brittle and rigid, made of iron like the railings that go all the way around the jardin, high black railings dipped in gold and shaped like spears that you cannot climb over.

The hospital was lit up yellow against the dark pine trees of Neuilly. There was a silver and glass entrance with a big revolving door. The people coming out looked like they'd just got off a flight from Dubai. Inside there was a bank of receptionists speaking English into telephone headsets. There was a pink marble floor and a cafe with potted palms. It looked more like a hotel than a hospital, only the guys sitting in the cafe had see-through dying skin and tubes coming out of their noses.

Maman was alone when we walked into her room. She was up high on a metal bed, talking on her phone. There was no sign of the baby. I wondered if she had given it away, the way she gives away her clothes when she doesn't want them any more.

'I know that, maman. I've told them already, they are taking her to the nursery tonight.' Her voice was tight. 'Listen I've got to go, Gabriel and Paul are here. Come tomorrow, not too early. I've got the consultant coming first thing.'

She put the phone down beside her bed, looked up at me and smiled; it was her big white smile. She was barefoot and stretched out with her dark hair spread against the pillow. Her nails were painted red; her black sunglasses were pushed to the top of her head. She looked like she was hanging out in a hotel room somewhere, taking a rest before she headed down to the pool. She wore a little grey top with thin straps, so her tanned shoulders were almost bare. The curve of her breasts showed, and her stomach was so flat that I wondered if there'd ever been a baby in there at all.

Even in the hospital, the magic was there. The air lay still against her skin and it was as if her every curve, every contour, every bone was made to be seen. She knows it's happening, that you are watching her. She's at ease with the deal: that she's the one who is and you are the one who admires. That is the way it has always been. I've seen photos of her when she was sixteen in blue denim, breaking boys' hearts. Sometimes I wonder if maman exists when there isn't someone there to look at her.

'My love,' she said, holding her arms out to me.

I took a step towards her, but Gabriel got there first. He kissed her on the mouth.

'How's that beautiful little girl of mine?' he said.

I waited until he backed away. I stepped forward and bent my head. Her lips were soft and cold against my forehead.

'My little Paul,' she said. I closed my eyes and breathed in the scalp beneath her hair. She smelled of jasmine. I put my arms around her neck, my hands underneath her hair, holding her to me until I felt her stiffen and she pulled away.

'We got stuck in the tunnel,' I said. 'I got claustrophobia. It was dark in the tunnel and there was all this red light from the brakes ahead and the speed dial on the car was glowing green in my eyes and everything was pushing down on me; I was suffocating and there were exhaust fumes and Gabriel was smoking a cigar so I couldn't breathe.'

'My poor baby,' she said, but she wasn't looking at me, she was searching through the bag that Gabriel had brought with him. 'Did you remember the cream, babe?' she said.

'Yeah, I remembered the cream.'

Someone had given her a big bouquet of pink roses. Pink like lingerie. They sat in a vase next to the television. There must have been thirty roses in that vase, tightly packed with masses of folded petals. The stems were strapped together with strands of raffia so they couldn't move; they made me think of the tunnel, of being trapped.

'Hey, Paul,' Gabriel said. 'Come and meet your sister.'

He walked over to a small room that was connected to my mother's room by a glass wall with a door. He pushed open the door and switched on the light.

'I don't want her waking up,' maman called out.

There was a crib in the glass room, I could see that now, a transparent Plexiglas crib that sat high up on a metal stand with wheels. They have the same cribs at the children's clothing boutique on the Rue de Tournon, down from the Jardin du Luxembourg. They put plastic dolls in those cribs at the shop. They dress the dolls in little blouses with buttons that shine like pearls and then they wrap them in cashmere blankets that smell of clementines.

Maman went shopping there all the time when she was pregnant. We used to go after I'd been to the orthodontist. It's where all the mothers in the 6ème go. The manageress would come over as soon as maman walked through the door. She was like a snake, watching maman from behind her big brown glasses.

'I'm so glad you came by,' she'd say, looking maman up and down, pausing, checking out her stomach, making her wait before she said: 'My god, Séverine, you still haven't put on any weight,' and maman purred to be told she was intact.

I would sit and watch the women shopping. They wore dark skinny trousers and high heels; they talked on their phones, they flicked their screens, they'd lean over the dolls and reach into the cribs and rub the baby cardigans between a thumb and finger. They had tanned ankles like maman.

'How was your day?' maman said now, she was head down and texting. She can run her business and her son from her mobile, that's what she tells people. 'What did you get in your maths?'

'She didn't give it back,' I said.

'She always gives it back on a Monday.'

'Paul,' Gabriel called out, 'you've got to see her fingers. Man, they're so cute.'

I didn't want maman finding out about my maths, so I went over to the glass room. There wasn't much in there. There was a washbasin and a yellow plastic changing mat; there was a medical chart hanging up. There was a pile of very small nappies to the left of the basin. There was Lou.

She was purple with an orange tinge and there were tiny white bubbles all over her nose. She was lying in the crib. Her eyes were closed. She didn't look like me. She didn't even look like maman. She was small, smaller than the plastic dolls in the boutique. She had black hair that didn't look like real hair; it looked like lots of feathers stuck onto a small purple and orange head.

Gabriel reached into the crib and picked her up.

'My little princess,' he said. He held her in his arms across his body. He held her like she was a rabbit. I turned away and came back out to where maman lay.

'She's purple,' I said.

'Yeah, that's just the way new-born babies look. Actually she looks better than you did when you were born, because she didn't get damaged on the way out. They lifted her out. You came out with a squashed head.'

'She's gonna break hearts,' Gabriel said as he came out of the glass room, still carrying the baby. 'Yes you are, my little Lou. You are going to be the most beautiful girl in Paris.'

Maman laughed out loud when he said that, like she thought it was funny. She reached up with her hand and tossed her hair so that it fell over one shoulder and she smiled at me and said:

'Hey, Paul, go stand by Gabriel and I'll take a photo.' When I didn't move she said, 'Don't sulk, be nice. Come on, do it for me, will you?'

I went to stand by Gabriel and Lou. Maman lay on the bed, watching us from over the top of her mobile, checking her screen to see how I looked, to see if I was the way she wanted me to be.

'Keep your chin up, Paul,' she said. 'Yeah, that's better.'

'When are you coming home?'

'I should be out Saturday. Hold her head, Gabriel, her head is flopping.'

'But that's in five days.'

She flicked across the photos on her screen. The baby started making noises, animal squeaks, and then she opened her eyes. How come she had dark blue eyes when maman's eyes were brown? And one of her eyes was staring at the other. She probably wasn't even maman's child.

'She's cross-eyed,' I said.

'It's normal, all babies are like that at first. Oh god, I knew she'd wake up, now she'll want a feed.' Maman was sending out the photos. 'You're gonna have to listen to me, Gabriel, I've done this before. Do you want to hold her, Paul?'

'No,' I said.

'Are you jealous?'

'No.'

'What is it then?'

'I'm hungry.'

'You're always hungry.'

The baby was whimpering now.

'Gabriel didn't bring me anything to eat.'

'Have some fruit.' She pointed to a bowl of waxy green apples and then she went back to sending her photos.

'I told papa,' I said.

'Told him what?'

'About the baby.'

She looked up then.

'Why the hell did you do that?'

'I didn't know it was a secret.'

'I didn't say it was a secret. I didn't want you to tell him, that's all.'

It was as if Lou sensed the tension, because she stopped snuffling and squeaking and started crying, real crying.

'What did you tell him?' maman asked.

I shrugged. 'I dunno. I just said, you know, the baby was born.'

'And?'

Lou screwed up her face and cried louder. It was a strange kind of wail; metallic and jerky.

'She's hungry,' Gabriel said, hoisting her onto his

shoulder. 'Poor baby, look at the way she's pecking my shoulder.'

'It's not time for a feed,' maman snapped. She turned back to me. 'What did he say?'

'Nothing,' I said. 'He didn't reply.'

Her mouth tightened.

'Typical,' she said, and then: 'You should go.'

'But I only just got here.'

'Yeah, but Gabriel's parents are coming and I need him to take you home now so that he can get back so I'm not sitting here entertaining them on my own. Gabriel, you need to take Paul.'

Gabriel was jogging around the room with his aviators on top of his head and Lou was snatching up her legs beneath her, wailing like she'd just been hit.

'I know, I know, honey, daddy's got to go, but he'll be back soon with *mamie* and *papi*.' He handed Lou to maman, but that only made the crying worse. Her skin was turning blackish purple; she took huge rasping breaths at the end of each cry, sucking in the air to fuel the next scream, making the room turn panicky.

'I need a nurse,' maman said. 'Where the hell is the nurse?' She pressed the red button by her bed.

'Let's go, Paul,' Gabriel called out, he was already by the door.

'When will I see you again?' I said to maman.

'Not tomorrow, you've got your tutor. Come Wednesday, come with Cindy, I'll get a taxi to pick you up after school,' she said, sticking a pacifier in Lou's mouth. Lou pushed it out a couple of times, then grabbed at it with her lips and sucked hard, opening her eyes wide.

'Who's gonna stay with me?'

'Cindy, of course, and Gabriel.'

'Gabriel?' He'd never stayed at our apartment without maman before.

'Yeah, Paul, that's me. Remember?' He made a face like I was stupid.

There was a loud knock and the door swung open before maman had a chance to say anything. It was Estelle. She stood in the doorway and threw back her head.

'Oh my god, Séverine. I could hear her screaming from the lift,' she said. 'Poor baby must be starving.'

She advanced on maman, her leopard-print blouse undone, her décolleté exposed for us all to see her tanned flesh, her turquoise medallion. Her mass of hair was curly and brown, spun gold by a hairdresser. She was weighed down by shopping bags and earrings that dangled and musk perfume that took up the whole room.

'She's adorable,' Estelle said. 'Look at her! She's too much.'

'Isn't she?' maman said. 'She's the dream baby. You can't imagine. She's too beautiful, *trop belle.*' She let the *o* of *trop* slide in her mouth so that it lasted for ages.

Everything is *trop* when maman speaks to Estelle: too cute, too sexy, too cool, *trop belle*, *trop beau*. Estelle is her best friend. They compete to see who can have the most *trop* in her life, who has the best lover, the best holiday, the best bikini, the best diet, the best divorce. Maman is more beautiful than Estelle and thinner, but Estelle is a man-eater. She's had sex with a fireman.

'I can't believe you gave birth this morning. Look at you! Don't tell me that gorgeous-looking doctor of yours gave you a little help with your stomach. I wish I'd done that. My god, you look like a young girl, doesn't she, Gabriel?'

She turned to Gabriel, who was still standing by the door.

'And, daddy, you don't look so bad either,' she said. 'You're as handsome as a god. Now, let me see her. I want to know which one of you the love child looks like.'

'Her daddy, of course.' Gabriel winked at Estelle.

Estelle saw me then, standing by the door.

'Why, Paul, darling, what are you doing hiding over there?'

She came towards me, grabbed me by the upper arms, and hugged me to her so that her hair was in my mouth and my face was in her breasts, my cheek thrust up against the metal edge of her medallion. She smelled of smoke and men and Paris.

'Not too jealous?' she said, looking me in the eye, before letting me go and handing me one of the shopping bags she was carrying. 'I bought you a present. Head-phones – you're gonna need them. I've got to warn you, Paul, babies are a pain in the arse. Max made me promise I'd never have another. But now I see her, I've got to tell you I'm feeling tempted. How's about it, daddy?' She winked at Gabriel.

'You guys should go,' maman said. She leaned over and pushed the red button again. 'Gabriel's parents are coming later to see the baby.'

'The grandparents?' Estelle smiled slyly. 'Doesn't that make you feel a little old, Gabriel?'

'Yeah, it feels kind of weird. Finding myself a dad, you know, I feel really different, it's like—'

'You need to go,' maman said, cutting him off. She swung her eyes towards the door.

'OK, babe,' he said.

'You too, Paul,' she said.

I thought perhaps maman would let me stay now that Estelle was here.

'But I only just got here,' I said again.

'*Oh là là*, big brother is not a happy boy.' Estelle pursed her lips and came back towards me, swinging her hips as she walked.

'Listen, Paul.' Her voice was gushy, like she had something nice to say. 'You've had your mother all to yourself all these years. You're a big boy now. You're gonna have to share her with the baby. You're gonna have to grow up.'

I looked over Estelle's shoulder to where maman lay; she was holding Lou while she checked her texts. I wanted maman to tell Estelle that it wasn't true, that I didn't have to share her with anyone.

'I'll see you Wednesday, my love,' maman said. She waved at me with the phone still in her hand.

Estelle stood there, hand on hip, green eyes hard, between me and maman.

'*Allez*, Paul.' Gabriel pulled at my sleeve.

I gave a last look to see if maman was watching.

'God, I could kill for a cigarette,' I heard Estelle say as I shut the door behind me.

2

The next day Cindy was waiting for me outside school, waiting in her shiny black bomber jacket with her bouncy ponytail and a packet of Prince Lu in her hand. It was the Prince Lu I love: creamy white icing sandwiched between two biscuits.

I tore open the packet and the corrugated cardboard inside and I ate them one after the other, pulling the biscuits apart and scraping the icing off with my front teeth. It stuck to my brace and I could taste it in the metal, vanilla and sweet. I pushed at it with my tongue for ages after.

We walked together along the Rue d'Assas. It goes on for ever that road, but I like it because it's the only road around here where I can almost see the horizon behind the spires in the distance, the other side of the river, beyond my reach. I ran my hand along the walls. I traced the horizontal furrows between the concrete slabs. I stared into the ground-floor windows, where the concierges live. I didn't see much. They put up net curtains or they close the white shutters to keep people like me from looking in. There were red geraniums in window boxes that smelled of hot earth.

The pharmacy on the corner had posters of gigantic

nits in the windows. They do it every year in September when you go back to school, the nit-treatment promotion; it's to frighten all the mothers. It's mostly families that live around here, families with kids. The streets don't look rich, but they are. Everyone wants to live here to be near the jardin and the schools. People make out like the Jardin du Luxembourg is this kind of fairy-tale place where kids run around pushing sail-boats with sticks. That's what estate agents say about this neighbourhood, that it's the setting for a dream childhood.

Cindy and I don't talk much, but it feels good when she is with me. She has kids, a girl and a boy, aged seven and nine. She left them behind in the Philippines when she came to France, and their dad looks after them. She works to send money home. She says that is the only way she can pay for them to go to school.

'So expensive, Paul, everything in the Philippines costs too much.'

I hadn't thought the Philippines would be expensive; I'd thought the Philippines would be poor and cheap, but Cindy says it costs loads to see a doctor there. Now she's got an aunt with a kidney problem so she sends her money too. Cindy's got no papers, so she can't go home, because if she goes home she can't come back. So she can't go to see her kids. She talks to them on Skype every day. She spends hours on Skype. All the mothers around here think their Filipinos are peasants or something; they think if these women weren't cleaning their kitchens with Mr Clean, they'd be working in a rice paddy. They don't know the

Filipinos are all out there skyping on their smartphones. Cindy has this big white Samsung that all the Filipinos have, and as soon as we get home she whips it out and hits the dial to chat to her kids. She's different when she speaks her own language. When she speaks English she is quiet and shy and she smiles more than she talks, but when she speaks Filipino she laughs out loud and she talks non-stop and she says '*mmm-mmn, wah, wah,*' and her voice rises and falls.

Cindy left me at the bottom of my dad's building where Rue de Babylone meets Rue Chomel. He lives in a big grey apartment building with huge windows. Some of the windows still had their summer blinds up, yellow and white striped awnings that make you think of the beach. Essie buzzed me up. She's my dad's Filipino. She's old, about fifty or so, and her face is kind of puffy. She opened the door wearing one of her fake Disney sweatshirts that said Sweet Posy across her breasts.

My dad wasn't in. I guessed he was still at his office in La Défense. He's got a big apartment for someone who lives all alone. He hasn't got much furniture, but it's supposed to look like that. In the salon there are two beige silk sofas and on either side of them are dark brown floor lamps with big papery beige lampshades. There is a mirror above the fireplace and a white ceiling with leaves that go all the way around and men's faces poking out in the corners. They give me the creeps.

There was a pile of fitness magazines stacked up neatly on the coffee table. Some were in French, some in English, but they were all pretty much the same, talking about diet and abs and how to build up open water swim training, that kind of thing. I flicked through them while I waited. There were pages and pages of biking shoes and Lycra shorts, bike gear, wetsuits, sunglasses and helmets. All the men were hard with steel thighs, tense calves and six-packs. 'We are all winners,' I remember that was one of the headlines.

Before he got into triathlons, my dad used to be crazy about tennis. He played three times a week; he used to obsess about his serve and volley and whether he could beat his brother, that was all he cared about. Then the year before he and maman split up, he began running 10k races; he got a trainer, ran a half-marathon, and then did the New York marathon. He took up biking. He bought an aquamarine Bianchi bike that cost 7,000 euros and he started biking at the weekends with the guys from the bank. It was one of the things that drove maman crazy; he would take off at 6 a.m. and not get back until midday. He'd walk in and get Cindy to cook him a massive plate of pasta with three chicken breasts lying on top, then he'd eat it, fall asleep for two hours, get up, take a shower, and go into the office.

He bought a rowing machine that he put in the garage down in the courtyard; he said it was good for stamina. He downloaded all these apps to track his fitness, his calories, his protein, his timing, his distances run, his distances cycled. He was constantly buying Lycra stuff and gadgets and gears, like the kit in the magazines, and there were packages arriving two or three times a week, things he'd bought on the Internet.

Then he said he wanted to bring his bike on holiday. We were going to Morocco with Estelle and her son and her new boyfriend. My dad bought a special hard case for the bike and he took it to the airport in a taxi; maman and I followed behind in another taxi with all the luggage. We had to get to the airport really early to get the bike specially checked in, and then when we landed they couldn't find it.

The lady from Air France kept ringing people all over the place and speaking in Arabic and my dad kept slamming his fist down on the counter, shouting: 'This is not possible!' I thought the lady was going to cry.

Maman was going crazy because Estelle had got an earlier flight and she was already at the Riad texting maman and sending her photos of the pool. And then these Arab guys kept coming by every ten minutes and asking us did we need a taxi.

Finally the bike case came round on the luggage belt, bumping along all alone and covered in red stickers marked, 'Security checked.' Everyone else from our flight had long gone.

'Your goddamn bike,' maman shouted as my father pulled it off the luggage belt. 'You care more about your bike than me.'

It took an hour and fifty minutes to drive to the Riad. My parents didn't talk in the limo, not once. This old guy in a white fez came out to greet us when we drove up; he took our bags and a lady came out carrying a tray of mint tea for my parents and lemonade for me. She poured the tea from a silver teapot, holding it up high so that the tea cascaded gold into the tiny glass below and the smell of mint was everywhere. It was beautiful, but only I was watching.

I liked the Riad. It was cool inside after the heat outside and the staff crept around on marble floors as if they didn't dare make a sound. There was a stone basin in the courtyard with big orange fish in it and a little fountain that sprinkled water all the time. But then maman found out Estelle had taken the lush white bedroom overlooking the swimming pool. It was the bedroom that was in all the photos maman had shown me when she booked the Riad. It had billowing white curtains, a four-poster bed and a huge white marble bath in the middle of the bathroom that you stepped down into. I remember in the photos there were red rose petals all over the bathroom floor and a sultry-looking babe lying on the middle of the bed wearing a white djellaba.

'I knew she'd do that,' maman said as she slammed the door to the smaller blue and white bedroom Estelle had left my parents. 'It's me that finds the Riad and organizes the holiday and Estelle just swans in and takes the best bedroom, all because of your bike. Your bike, your ego, Philippe.' She shouted the last words, punching them out as she threw her handbag down onto the bed.

'Your friend, your problem,' my father said. He was on his phone and he didn't bother looking up.

Estelle was standing at the bottom of the stairs when maman and I went back down.

'Listen, darling, you don't mind about the bedroom, do you?' Estelle said. She was barefoot and smelled of coconut oil; her red bikini was wet and heavy against her skin. Her eyes were like green marbles watching maman. She'd had her breasts done after her divorce, which meant she now had enormous tits that she showed off whenever she could. There were water droplets caught between them, skating down her oily cleavage.

'Only I need to be by Max's bedroom,' she said, rolling her eyes, 'to keep an eye on him.' Max is her gaming freak of a son who spends his life on Grand Theft Auto and then goes to see a psychiatrist twice a week to talk about it. He'd failed all his written assessments and he was being made to stay down a year.

'Of course not, *ma belle*,' maman said. 'You absolutely need to watch out for him. Staying down a year, what a nightmare.' Maman sucked in her breath, 'How do you think that happened?'

Estelle flinched when maman said that.

Other than hanging out by the pool, there was nothing to do at the Riad. It was too hot to do anything. Max spent the week gaming in the dark in the cinema room. Estelle spent the week draping her tits off the side of her sun lounger and getting her boyfriend to take photos of her on her phone. Maman lay by the pool texting her friends who were staying in Marrakech.

'We should have stayed in town, Philippe,' she said on

the second day. 'I'm bored. Estelle is doing my head in, panting all over that photocopier salesman. I told you we should have stayed in Marrakech, but you wanted to play golf.'

My dad got up at 5 a.m. every morning to go biking before the heat of the day. He kept telling me to play tennis.

'You should be out there on the court,' he said on the fourth day.

'I'm too tired,' I said.

'From what?' he said. 'You don't do anything.'

Every afternoon a lady brought Moroccan cakes to us where we lay by the pool. That was the best bit of the holiday. There were loads of pastries: round and sweet, foreign-tasting, made of coconut and pistachios and almonds. There was one that looked like folded hair dripping in honey. That was my favourite. Maman lounged by the water reading her magazines and complaining about the air-conditioning or how much my dad was training. My dad was on conference calls or swimming lengths, biking, or playing golf with a client. I hardly saw him. That was our last holiday together.

My dad's salon looks out onto a park, the small one right by Le Bon Marché. I like staring out over the rooftops at the sky; I like the red sign of the Hôtel Lutetia lit up on the roof of the hotel. The Nazis took over the hotel during the Occupation; they tortured people in there. Our teacher told us that.

He's lucky, my dad, that there are no apartments opposite him. He doesn't have to look into other people's lives. I guess he sees people down below in the park, but not close up, not zoomed in, not in his face, not watching them in their underpants after a bath; he's not listening to their arguments echoing in the courtyard, hearing the cork pop when they open a bottle of wine. He's not living their lives.

He can see the sky from his apartment, the whole sky, all around him, not just a lid of sky that seals the courtyard tight.

Maman hates that my dad lives here. She tells everyone she loves the Jardin du Luxembourg and the neighbourhood, but I know she and my dad moved there only to be near the school I didn't get into. She would love to be here, by the shops and cafes of Saint-Germain, she would love to be closer to the Flore. She hates that my dad can do his grocery shopping at La Grande Épicerie, which is the swanky food department of Le Bon Marché, where they sell little blocks of sugar shaped like the Eiffel Tower. Only it isn't him that does the grocery shopping, it's Essie.

'You wan' a banana?' I jumped at the sound of Essie's voice. She was standing right behind me. She always does that. 'I get you something to eat,' she said. I followed her into the kitchen. There's never anything worth eating in my dad's fridge, just energy drinks and cold quinoa.

'What time will he get back?' I asked.

Essie shrugged. 'Always working,' she said as she peeled the banana, 'he works too hard.'

I went into his bedroom. I opened his wardrobe: navy-blue suits and shirts for work. I opened his drawers: grey underpants, black socks, grey socks, a black Hermès belt maman had given him. There were a couple of books by his bedside, one about taxes and the other about nutrition for triathletes. I went through all the cupboards in his bathroom, all the shelves. I found a bottle of shampoo from London that said 'managing hair loss' on the front.

I went out and along the corridor. I opened the door to the laundry room. There were seven office shirts hanging from a metal frame on the ceiling, and a pair of black running trousers were dangling there, waiting for legs. Nothing else, just Essie's cleaning products stacked up on the side and the white floor tiles pristine and polished underfoot.

I went into the salon. I sat back down on the sofa. I was looking around for the remote when I noticed my dad's iPad jutting out from underneath the coffee table. Usually he keeps it in a really expensive ostrich-skin cover that maman gave him for Christmas one year. But it was lying there naked without a cover.

I slipped off the sofa and onto my knees and then I crawled until the iPad was beneath me. There were fingerprints all over the glass. My finger found the indented button; I pushed it and the screen came alive. It was a photo of my dad on his bike. A photo of him with his helmet and his black sunglasses and his white Lycra, head low over the handlebars, jaw thrusting, racing to win.

I didn't know his code to get in. I tried some numbers; I was breathing hard, I don't know why. Think of four numbers he would choose, it can't be that difficult. I tried again. I wanted to know what he kept behind that glass.

Then the front door opened and I heard his voice. I found the top right-hand switch; I pushed it so there was only black glass and then I slid the iPad back under the coffee table. I got to my feet.

'You're doing great, Philippe,' a man said in English, 'your finishing speed is picking up.'

I walked out into the corridor.

'Paul,' my father said; he looked surprised to see me. We hadn't spoken since I texted him about the baby. 'I forgot you were coming.' There was sweat running down his body, from his face to his chest, from his calves to the floor. The veins jutted out around his throat and legs.

'This is Todd,' he said, speaking English and pointing to the blond man by his side. 'Todd, this is my son, Paul.'

Todd had shoulders that were too wide for a corridor. He had a body that he must have to exercise all the time to stop it from running wild. He was more animal than man. He made my dad look slight in comparison; he made my dad look French and narrow-framed, like he sat at a desk all day, like he came from a long line of men who wore suits, which he did.

'Hey, Paul,' Todd said. 'Nice to meet you.' He looked

me in the eye as he shook my hand. His hand was large and damp, powerful around mine. He spoke with an Australian accent. 'Your dad has told me all about you.'

'He has? What did he say?'

'What did he say?' Todd laughed, a big laugh so that I could see inside his mouth. 'Well, for a start, he told me you speak great English.'

I looked at my dad. His cheeks were flushed. He looked down at his phone. Last month he'd sent maman an email complaining about my English, telling her I needed a tutor.

'Todd's my new trainer,' my father said, without looking up. 'He's getting me ready for the Ironman.'

'Yeah,' Todd said. 'I'm taking your dad up a notch, working on his performance. Hey, Philippe, we should look at those stats before I get going.'

Dad started tapping on his screen.

'I'm faster than I was Friday, I'm faster on the first half; I still lost time on those last four ks.'

They stood in the corridor with their heads bent over the screen, the hair on their forearms, the blond hair of the animal man and the black hair of the banker man, close but not touching. They stood in silence as their sweat dripped onto the floor and I stood apart from them, watching.

'Yeah, next time we'll do it long and slow, then maybe forty-eight hours later take the pace right up, fast and furious. We need to build speed and stamina. That's the way you'll take Didier.'

He said Didier in his Australian accent so I wondered at first what he was talking about, then I realized he meant the guy at the bank who works with my dad. My dad was always plugging in Didier's times and trying to work out how to get past him.

'I better shoot,' Todd said. 'Nice meeting you, Paul.' He gave my hand another crunch and then he put his hand on my dad's shoulder.

'You text me, OK, Philippe? Keep it steady, we'll run Thursday. Have a great one.'

My dad opened the door for him.

'You too,' my dad said smiling.

He closed the door and turned back to me, still smiling.

The corridor was empty without Todd.

'They want me back at the office for a meeting. Did you eat already?' my dad said.

Essie came out of the kitchen and into the corridor; she dropped to her knees and started wiping up the sweat with a damp cloth.

'There's nothing to eat,' I said.

'There's quinoa. Essie can heat you up some quinoa.'

'I hate that stuff.'

'It would do you good,' he said, heading to the kitchen.

'I hate stuff that does me good.'

'You need to get over that.' He stirred dark green powder into a glass of water. 'How's your maths?' He made a face as he took his first gulp.

'OK.'

'Any results?' He was checking his phone.

'Three in the last homework. But it wasn't my fault because one of the questions didn't make sense.'

'Three? Three out of twenty? How is that even possible?'

'Everyone said it was way too hard and that the questions were really confusing.'

'I thought you were having tutoring. I thought that guy was coming twice a week. Hughes.'

'Hugo. He is,' I said. I felt the panic rise and catch in my throat, like a lift getting stuck between floors.

'Shit, and you're still getting three with a tutor?' He was angry again, the way he used to be when I was in CM2 and trying for senior school, when he thought I still stood a chance.

'You don't try hard enough, Paul. That's your problem, not enough effort. Life takes application to succeed. You have to work at it.'

He looked out of the window. His chest rose and fell. It just takes the word maths to set him off. He turned back to me.

'So,' he said, 'is she happy?' His jaw was still wired tight. I shrugged.

'She said she's the perfect baby,' I said.

'I bet.'

'She told Estelle that she felt different this time; she felt ready.'

He made a sound like he had swallowed something bitter.

'That's rich coming from the woman who swore she'd never have another baby,' he said.

I wondered if it was the baby that made him angry, or the man she'd had it with, a man who was younger than him, who played in a band, who had hair that didn't fall out in the shower.

'She says having a girl is different,' I said.

'Yeah, right. You mean more clothes to buy, more shopping.'

'Less complicated.'

'Than what?'

'Than me, I guess.'

He stared at me for a couple of seconds, but it was an empty stare, like he'd already forgotten what we were talking about, and then we heard an email come in on his phone and he looked down to read it.

'I should take a shower,' he said. He started towards the door and then he laughed. 'Hey, I almost forgot. I've got my own new arrival' – he smiled as his thumb smoothed the screen of his phone – 'my own pretty baby.' He handed me the phone so I could see the picture.

A dark grey Porsche 911 lit up the screen.

'Too beautiful,' I said.

'Don't believe them, Paul, when they tell you money can't buy you happiness.'

I stroked the screen. There were lots of pictures, close-ups of grey leather seats, the curve of the bonnet, a shot with the driver's door open, then a picture of the steering wheel and a close-up of the red, black, and gold crest of the Porsche with a rearing horse at its centre.

'Turbo cabriolet, maximum speed 315 kilometres per hour,' he said. 'I couldn't resist.'

'Can we go for a drive?'

'Not right now, I've got a deal on, they're waiting for me at the office. But sure, yeah, this weekend, why not?'

'I'm with maman this weekend,' I said.

'Well, some other time then.'

I stroked the screen again and there was a woman staring up at me. She was Asian-looking, not like Cindy, another kind of Asian. She was young. I can't tell ages but she was younger than my dad. Twenty-something, I think. She had silvery eyelids and glittery lips and her black hair was slicked back. She was smiling at me like she had something that she knew I wanted.

'Who's that?' I said with the phone still in my hand.

'Who?' My dad looked at his upside-down phone.

'Her,' I said. 'Who is she?'

He leaned across and took back the phone. His face was shut.

'She's just some girl,' he said.

3

The rain looked faint from inside the station, but there were a million more raindrops than in Paris. We were wet by the time we got to the minivan. Our taxi driver stood waiting in a polo shirt, making out it was just a passing shower. I got in the back of the van. Maman got in next to me.

'God, I hate Brittany,' she said, looking out at all the other Parisians queuing for taxis and wishing they had gone abroad. 'It's the end of the world.'

Everywhere we went now, we needed a truck to fit Lou and all her kit. She had a massive pram that you had to snap apart to get into the boot, a baby seat for the car, a sterilizer, nappies, cream for her bottom, cream for her face, baby bottles, and tins of milk powder. She had to have special bottles because she had colic and a special liquid to squirt down her throat to stop the colic. She had a ton of clothes because she was always being sick down herself.

It took the driver ages to pack it all in. It was hot inside the car, the windows were steamed up and Lou was screaming and turning red and the driver had on Radio Nostalgie playing some old person's love song. All Lou did was scream, drink milk, and sleep. She didn't actually do anything else. Cindy spent all her time looking after her now, taking her to the paediatrician, taking her for walks, bathing her, changing her, feeding her bottles. Maman was obsessed with the amount of milk Lou drank. She made Cindy keep all the bottles Lou drank from throughout the day, and when maman got back from work she went into the kitchen and picked up every bottle to inspect how much milk was left.

'She needs to finish the bottle, Cindy. I've told you. You've got to insist.' She said the same thing every night.

'You're from Paris?' the taxi driver asked now. He had one hand on the wheel, both eyes on maman.

'Yes,' maman said. She didn't look up from her phone.

It was the October Toussaint school holidays, which meant all the shops had those flowers outside their windows, the flowers that I hate: purple or orange buttons that open into spiky petals with green leaves that smell of darkened forests. On All Saints' Day people put pots of them on relatives' graves.

Maman was staring out at the tall dripping pine trees and the blank faces of the shuttered villas along the avenues. It looked like it had been raining for ever. The autumn sky was dull and overcast. It was two in the afternoon, but it felt like six o'clock.

'So what will you do here?' the driver asked.

'Thalassotherapy,' she said.

The taxi driver sighed. 'Madame will go home even more beautiful than before.'

Maman looked up then and smiled. You could see the

pink of her tongue between her teeth. She ran her hand through her hair.

'You're too kind,' she said.

The taxi driver blinked and swallowed. She can do that to you, maman; she can make you think she is in love with you. She does it all the time to all kinds of people, to the valet at Le Bon Marché when he parks her car, to the guy at the ski-lift when he lets her jump the queue, to the black guy who cleans her car in the underground car park on Avenue Marceau. 'What would I do without you, Marcel?' she says to him when he hands her back her keys.

She has a deep voice and dark brown eyes and skin that is olive like my dad's and long hair and long legs and a large diamond engagement ring that shines like a light bulb and that she wears even though they aren't together any more. She gets a table in restaurants where they say it is fully booked and she gets people to give her great rooms in hotels, and she gets on flights when there are no more seats.

The driver turned into the gold-and-white gates of the hotel. It was a big cream-coloured building with a dark grey slate roof and balustrades painted brick red.

'You are not alone,' he said.

There were cars double-parked all around the sweep of the drive, Jaguars, Porsches, Mercedes and Range Rovers; rich guys' cars with '75' Paris number plates. A doorman rushed out with a large umbrella. He led us through the revolving doors past about twenty pushchairs lined up against a wall.

'This is our other car park,' he said, wheeling Lou's pram into position. A young woman at reception checked us in. She was pretty like an air-hostess, with red lipstick and a red neckerchief and her hair held up in a fat bun on top of her head. Her name was Gwénaëlle; it said so on her badge.

'Are you going to Kids' Club?' she asked me. She could smile and keep her eyes wide open at the same time. 'You will love Kids' Club. We have so many fun Halloween activities to do!' Only someone who has never done Kids' Club would say that. 'Any dinner reservations, madame?' she asked. She couldn't stop smiling.

'I'll dine with my son tonight. My husband is arriving late from Paris.'

I checked out the lounge area while maman filled in the forms. There were heavy glass chandeliers and big black statues of fat women parked around the lounge. Steam was coming off the outdoor pool. 'This way.' The porter showed us up to our rooms on the fifth floor. Piped music was coming out of the television when we went into our room, and it said, 'Welcome Monsieur and Madame Lemaire' on the screen. I wondered why my mother kept telling everyone she was married. I switched to MTV.

'You're in here with Lou and Cindy. Our bedroom is just down the corridor,' maman said. 'Cindy, I'm going down for a treatment. Paul, if you're going to snack, make it fruit. We'll go for supper when I get back.'

'I thought it started tomorrow,' I said.

'That's the thalasso; this is a treatment. I need to have some treatments before I can have the thalassotherapy.'

She went off downstairs and I lay on my bed and watched TV. Cindy unpacked the bags. Then she opened the door. She had Lou in her arms.

'I go down the hall for your mother's clothes,' she said.

I got up and went to stand by the window. It had stopped raining. It was low tide. The beach was vast and long, and the sea was far away. There were no waves, just parallel lines of sky and sea and beach. It looked like you could punch your fist through the grey sky at the back of the horizon.

The hotel had left a deflated beach ball on one of the beds as a welcome gift, like I was aged five. I blew it up and threw it around the room for a bit. I remembered a ball like that, only it was green. I remembered jumping into a hotel pool and shouting, 'Watch me,' at my dad, who was sitting by the pool reading a pink newspaper.

I had a poke around the minibar. I ate a mini-box of Pringles. I sucked my fingers and shoved them down to the bottom of the tube to get up all the green and white dust. I ate a Toblerone. It didn't taste too good after the Pringles. I gamed. I waited.

I must have fallen asleep because next thing I knew maman walked back through the door.

'Where's Cindy?' she asked. She'd had her hair done so that it swung from side to side when she walked.

'She went to unpack,' I said.

'You've got to get up, they finish serving in five minutes.'

There were photos all along the corridor, black and white photos of white people having thalassotherapy treatments, a guy with water crashing down on his shoulders, a woman with black pebbles running down her back, then the same man and woman wrapped in white towels lying side by side on beds with their eyes closed looking like they never said: 'Fuck you, I'm leaving.' There were photos of boys and girls on the beach, fishing in rock pools with fishing nets on a stick and wearing Petit Bateau yellow oilskins. You never catch any fish with nets like those. It's just the kind of lame activity they make you do at Kids' Club.

'Paul, hurry,' maman called from the lift. I stepped inside.

'Oh my god, what was I thinking?' she said aloud as the doors closed. 'What am I doing here?'

I wasn't sure if she was expecting me to reply or if she was even speaking to me. The two frown lines between her eyes were coming back. She has injections to paralyse them, but after a while they come back, a track in the forest, stronger than her. She was looking at me strangely. She leaned forward a little.

'Have you been eating Pringles?'

'No.'

'Liar,' she said. The lift doors opened.

The corridor to the dining room was pale grey and the

carpet was the colour of red wine and we could hear children shouting from inside the dining room and I thought, she's not going to like this. We walked into a massive room with all these kids screaming and big round tables with white tablecloths and really young waiters looking like they'd lost control and parents sitting at the table looking like they were waiting for someone to come and make it all all right. And then I heard maman breathe a sigh of relief and she said:

'Oh thank god for that.'

She waved to someone on the other side of the room and said, 'Carla's sister's here. Over there, sitting at the table with the baby.' There were loads of women sitting at tables with babies.

'Over there,' maman said, trying not to point. 'Valérie, see her? The blonde. That's Carla's sister.'

I looked around the room at all the people. It was weird how many I recognized. It was as if everyone who hangs out at the Jardin du Luxembourg had decided to leave Paris and move to this dining room in La Baule. All the Rive Gauche beautiful people were there. The woman who jogs round the jardin all day doing tiny steps like she's a geisha, whose kids go to my school, she was sitting at a table, dressed in black and fluorescent-pink running kit. There was an actress whose kids go to the Rue Madame. She's always hanging out by the playground at the jardin; she wears thin cotton dresses that lap at her body and all the dads at my old junior school used to try and hit on her even though she must be forty.

And there was Scarlett. Scarlett from school. Scarlett Lacasse. Here in La Baule. She'd just joined our school in September. I remember her first day. She walked into chemistry with a savage smile on her face, like we were a bunch of losers and she was our queen. She sat looking at her phone until the teacher shouted at her to put it away and then she tossed it in her bag with a shrug. I'd never spoken to her.

She started going out with Stéphane in her first week and all the girls hated her because they wanted him. I remember I was in the jardin with Guillaume and Pierre when Scarlett and Stéphane stepped through a gap in the hedgerow where we were sitting. They walked hand in hand, not talking, just looking cool together. They didn't look at us. Stéphane had on his red Nike high-tops and a black hoodie. His hair was long and dark and curly and his high-tops were undone so the laces trailed in the dust. Scarlett was wearing tight black-and-red leopard-print jeans and a grey hoodie that said 'Brooklyn'. She didn't look like the other girls in our year. She had wild hair that flew around her face. Stéphane pulled her to him and they started kissing, right there in front of us, opening their mouths wide, shoving their tongues back and forth, in and out, like they were digging for gold.

We watched as Stéphane moved his right hand up under Scarlett's top and he pushed at her breasts.

'He's too lucky,' Pierre said.

'Anyone could have her,' Guillaume said with bitterness.

But none of us had.

And now here she was, in the same dining room as me in La Baule. She was sitting opposite a man and a woman. I guessed they were her parents. But they were not the parents Scarlett Lacasse should have had. She should have had rock-star parents, a skinny dad who wore black jeans and black sunglasses and made movies and a mum who was a TV presenter and drove a jeep. There was no way the old guy sitting opposite Scarlett was a film director. He wore reading glasses that had no frames, just a metal bridge over his thin nose and metal arms through his thin grey hair. He kept pressing his fingers together when he spoke like he was the pope. And the woman didn't look 6ème arrondissement at all, not rock-chick like maman or Estelle; she looked like she went to Mass where my grandparents go to Mass in Neuilly. She was wearing a navy-blue polo-neck sweater. I bet she had one of those nylon handbags maman hates. I bet she drove a great big Peugeot people-carrier. Maybe Scarlett was adopted.

'How are you, *ma belle?*' a woman at the table next to us called out to maman. It must have been some kind of sign, because all at once all these other women surged from around the room over to our table and kissed maman and said, Oh my god I can't believe you are here, when did you get here, how long are you staying, where's the baby, which treatment are you doing, you've lost weight, you look great, oh my god Séverine if you lose any more weight you'll disappear.

I went over to the buffet and piled my plate high with

everything the hotel had for kids' supper, really skinny fries covered in salt, ham rolled up into pink tubes, hunks of baguette and a big slab of Breton butter with salt crystals buried in it. I kept looking over at the dessert table. I couldn't believe it; there were gigantic chocolate and coffee éclairs and great big bowls of sweets, caramel Carambars and fraises Tagadas. I went over and stuffed some in my pockets just in case some of the young kids got in first and took them all.

When I got back to the table maman was revved up to go like it was a party. A fat-cat guy with slicked black hair and a tan moved in on her straightaway, telling her how great she looked, what a body she had. I was trying to shove fries in my mouth before maman stopped me. She must have known him from Paris.

'So are you here all alone, Séverine?' he asked as he pulled up a chair and sat down close to her. I could smell his after-shave from where I sat.

'Of course not, Serge,' maman said. 'I'm here with my son, Paul,' she pointed towards me, 'and I've got a new baby called Lou.'

'I didn't know,' he said without looking my way. He kept chewing on an unlit cigar, chewing as if it were a steak. He had dark brown suede shoes with no socks on; he had black hairs around his ankles, black hairs at his neck and his chest. I bet he had hairs in his ears; he was a hairball. He had a stomach that hung over the crotch of his dark denim jeans. He must look bad without his clothes on. He leaned across the table.

'Where's your new boyfriend, Séverine? Don't tell me he's left you all on your own.'

'Gabriel's got a gig tonight,' maman said. That was a lie. He was at a rehearsal, not a gig. I knew that for a fact because maman had spent the whole week telling him he should miss his rehearsal so he could come with us on the train.

'He's catching the late train,' maman said, 'he'll be here tonight.'

'Too bad,' he said. 'So what will you do while you're waiting?'

'Oh, you needn't worry about me, Serge.' Maman lifted her hair, which was loose around her shoulders, and her breasts rose as she tipped her head back a fraction. She let her hair fall down against her shoulders with a bang. 'I'm gonna catch up on my beauty sleep,' she said.

The fat cat laughed out loud; he laughed and laughed and when he stopped he said:

'Ah, Séverine, you always were the goddamn tease.'

I looked over at Scarlett. I wondered if she'd seen me. I wondered if she knew my name. She had on the black denim jacket that she wore to school and she was curled up over the phone in her hands. She is not beautiful, Scarlett, but she wears bras that make her breasts stand high up on her chest and she wears T-shirts that drop down low and all the boys are after what they think they can get. She didn't look my way.

'Serge.' A woman was standing by our table with a little girl at her side. 'Zélie needs the toilet.'

The girl was frowning at me like I was to blame. Her bottom jaw was too big for her face. It was her father's jaw.

'Can't you take her?' the fat cat said without looking away from maman.

'I'm feeding the baby,' the woman said.

'I'm bursting,' the girl said.

'I heard you.' The fat cat pushed back his chair and got up, but he kept looking at my mother as he moved off.

'Who is he?' I asked maman.

'Serge? Oh, I've known him for ever.' She laughed. And then her phone rang.

'Yes, my love.' Her voice was breathy. 'We're having dinner. Yeah, actually, it's fun, much better than I thought. It is not like Dinard, thank god. There are loads of people I know. Carla's sister is here, Valérie, you know? You're gonna like it.'

She was laughing as she spoke, taking fries from my plate, looking around at the tables, at the people, little sparks of light flying off her eyes and into the room. Scarlett was staring out of the window and into the darkness.

'Why not?' maman asked. She stopped taking my fries. 'You told me it finished early.'

There was a pause as Gabriel said something. Then maman said:

'What do you mean?'

I imagined Gabriel, pink lips close to the phone, tail between his legs, talking his way out of the situation. But whatever he was saying wasn't working. She gave him four seconds before she cut him off.

'You know what, Gabriel, you better be on that train tomorrow morning. I am not sitting in La Baule with your child without you. Get your arse down here. Understood?' She pressed end.

'*Connard*,' she said. A message flew in immediately. She picked up the phone to read it.

'*Connard*,' she said again and slammed the phone back down on the tablecloth.

'He's still at the studio,' maman said. 'He's not even at the station.' She pushed the phone away from her. 'I don't believe that guy.' She ran her hands through her hair. She looked around the room; she watched to see who Valérie was talking to. She checked her phone again. I saw Serge walking back to his table, looking over at maman.

I imagined Gabriel with his band, sharing a couple of beers with the guys at the end of the rehearsal. And then I imagined him kick-starting his scooter and heading over to the Boulevard Saint-Germain, parking up on the Rue Saint-Benoît and strolling down the road to the Flore with that smile on his lips. He'd check out the tables in the front, share a joke with the waiter standing at the door, take a seat out on the terrasse, light his cigar, and order a beer, still tucked up in his Moncler padded jacket with the cream scarf tied around his neck. He'd send a bleeding-heart text to maman while he watched the girls go by on the Boulevard Saint-Germain, one by one, and he'd drink his beer, sucking the froth from the bristle above his lip. That is what he does.

He'd be here tomorrow. I was sure of it. He's like a

dog, Gabriel, racing around the park, pissing against tree trunks, sniffing at all the girls, looking up their skirts until my mother yanks the lead tight, jerks the collar with her wrist, and he comes flying back to her side.

4

They broke up at the dead end of August, when I was eleven years old. My parents had sent me away to my grandparents for the week. My cousins were there too, my father's elder brother Xavier's three sons. They are great at tennis and they are great at maths; they are everything you are supposed to be.

My grandmother signed us up for a tennis camp in the mornings and I got put in the bottom group. It was full of girls who screamed every time a ball came their way. I had this fat woman of a coach, who stood at the baseline and fired balls around the court from a machine and told me to move my butt when she had obviously never moved hers.

In the afternoons we went to the beach and I lay out in my clothes on the sand with my headphones on while my cousins swam and played football barefoot. My grandmother kept seeing people she knew on the beach and introducing us as 'my grandchildren.' She said it like she owned us or like we were some kind of trophy, except when she introduced me, then I saw her eyelids flicker. At night my cousins played cards or told stories about their school in the 16ème where you get taught by Jesuits and everyone needs glasses from working too hard. That's where my dad and his brother went to school. I had nothing to say. I sat in the salon and gamed.

By the end of the week my grandmother had had enough of me; she kept saying I needed to do something about my eating, that it wasn't normal for a boy of my age. I hid the packets of sweets behind my bed, but she found two empty boxes of barbecue Pringles in my tennis bag and she told me I had no self-control.

The night before I was due to go home, she got a call from her friend Diane asking her to play in a golf competition the next morning. Diane was the social queen of Dinard. She was some kind of countess and her villa was older and chicer than everyone else's. I heard my grandmother using her grand piano voice to talk to her on the phone. It was the same voice she used when she spoke to the butcher.

The next morning at eight she came rushing into my bedroom wearing all her Lacoste golfing clothes. She was in a fluster. She told me I had to get up and get dressed straightaway, as plans had changed and she was putting me on an earlier train back to Paris. She drove fast out of the drive, bashing the pink hydrangea heads to get me to the station. We went past the beach. The little blue-and-white-striped tents were lined up for the day. There were waves breaking on the empty sand, seagulls sorting out their feathers in the morning breeze and I could smell the sea. I had that feeling you get in the morning on the beach when no one has arrived and the waves are bright and the sand is smooth and damp, untouched. It made me sad to go, leaving all that sky.

'Don't blame me,' she said as she parked in a disabled bay right outside the station doors. 'I can't say no to Diane.'

Her eyes were shiny with excitement beneath her red-and-blue-checked sun visor. She pulled out a twenty-euro note from her wallet and frowned at me.

'I've tried calling your mother, but she won't pick up.' She looked guilty then as she handed over the money. 'Don't spend it all on sweets.'

She couldn't wait to get away. I watched her reverse out in my grandfather's powder-blue Mercedes; it's got assisted parking because she's so bad at it. I didn't care that she wanted to get rid of me.

The train from Dinard was packed with grandparents taking their grandchildren back to Paris. It was the Saturday before schools started. I hadn't heard from my parents all week except for two texts from maman saying, 'Are you OK?' I texted her on the train but she didn't reply. I texted Cindy telling her I was coming home.

Cindy was there on the platform at Montparnasse waiting for me. The station was hot and it was hard to breathe. A loud bell was ringing as we walked all the way down the platform, so we didn't try to talk. Outside, the tarmac was sticky underfoot. The taxi smelled of fake peaches; it had dirty nylon seats and windows that you had to wind down with a broken handle. The driver was sullen and white. They're always angry in August because you've been away and they haven't. After the blue of Dinard, everything was grey. The shops and apartment buildings were lined up and waiting for me on the Boulevard Montparnasse. The pavements and people, the traffic; nothing had changed. It was all just the way it had always been and that made me sad.

We stopped on our road and Cindy got out a fifty-euro note to pay for the short journey home.

'I'm not a bank,' the taxi driver said.

'Have you got any change, Cindy?' I asked.

She shook her head and giggled, which made it worse.

He swore and slapped the steering wheel.

'Tell her this isn't China.'

'She's not from China,' I said, 'she's from the Philippines.'

He turned around so that he was facing us. He was snarling like a dog.

'I don't care if she's from fucking Mars, she should go back to where she came from.'

I grabbed my bag and got out. The seat sagged where I had sat. He flung the change at Cindy as she was getting out of the car, then he roared off down the road. I turned to go in.

The street was silent again, empty. Nothing moved in the heat. There was a removal van parked right outside our apartment building. The back was open and there was a pile of grey blankets in the van, each blanket had a red stripe and they had been folded so that the red stripe went all the way up the pile.

Upstairs I found the door to our apartment wide open. There were four black guys in the salon wearing red polo shirts and sweating. They were carrying my dad's desk across the parquet. On the polo shirts it said: 'Corporate and Executive Removals'.

At first I thought maman must have persuaded my dad to get rid of the furniture she didn't like, but then I saw that there were cardboard boxes as well, a stack of them over by the window, waiting. I went over to them. There was a sticker on each box that said Monsieur Philippe Deslandes. Underneath my father's name someone had printed an address that was not our address. I touched a sticker. The word 'salon' was underlined three times in black marker, like it had some special meaning.

I called my dad on the phone and he said, 'Where are you?' and I said, 'At the apartment.' He said, 'What are you doing there?' and I said, 'Grandmother put me on an early train.'

'*Merde*,' he said. And then, 'I'll come.'

I waited for him out on the balcony. I looked down at the street; I looked down at the roofs of the parked cars. I stood and swayed. The air was stale, heavy with the month of August. I felt sick. I waited until I saw his dark hair below. He didn't come up. He called me from his phone down on the pavement. I watched him do it. I took the stairs down; I ran my hand along the cool brass banister, around and around, tracing a spiral, looking down into the empty space and the black and white marble below, until I reached the ground floor. I opened the heavy wooden door and stepped out onto the pavement; it was hard to move through the still, thick heat.

We walked along the road for a bit and then he told me as we turned onto the Rue d'Assas. He told me he had found an apartment near Le Bon Marché, that he would buy me an Xbox so I could play on it when I came to stay. He told me he was leaving.

'We've decided to take a break,' he said as we walked along side by side. 'Your mother and I.'

'What from?'

'From each other.'

'Why?' I said.

'I don't know, Paul. Maybe we are not happy people to begin with.'

'What about me?'

'What about you?'

'Are you taking a break from me?'

He stopped then and said: 'Of course not, Paul, of course not.' But he didn't smile and put his arms around me.

He said: 'You'll carry on living with your mother during the week and then some weekends you'll come and stay with me. We haven't worked out how often you'll come yet.'

We turned down by the Lycée Montaigne. School hadn't started. There were no children hanging around outside; instead, there were big black tour buses from Eastern Europe. The drivers were standing on the pavement, eating baguettes and speaking a language I didn't understand. They had cruel bodies like wrestlers and they wore big gold buckles on their belts. I wondered why my parents were splitting up now at the end of summer. I wondered what it was that broke them.

We crossed into the jardin, so that we were walking under the alley of trees, in and out of light and shadow. The leaves were brown and dried up. They were dying where they hung. The flowers in their beds looked like they were tired of the summer; they were waiting to be pulled up, to be taken away. It was strange to think that people were still at the beach, still on holiday, and here in the jardin, autumn had begun. My phone rang.

'*Chéri*,' maman said, 'where are you?'

'At the jardin.'

She was calling from her car. I could hear her voice up against the windscreen and a siren driving past.

'What are you doing there? You weren't supposed to get in until this afternoon.'

'I got an early train.'

'An early train?'

'Grandmother made me. She was playing in a golf competition.' My voice was crushed flat. 'Diane asked her to play. She said she couldn't say no to Diane.'

'What the hell was she doing putting you on an earlier train without telling me?'

'She said she called you, but you didn't pick up. I called

you too, but you didn't answer. I left you loads of messages.' I wanted maman to know she should have been there.

'*Putain* that woman; she changed the plan. She did it on purpose. She changed the plan. I'm going to call your father.'

'He's here,' I said. 'He's here with me.'

She lost it then. I remember thinking she must have looked strange in the traffic, shouting in her car; the people next to her must be staring at her. Maman doesn't usually mind being stared at.

'Put him on the phone!' she shouted. 'Put your father on the phone.'

My dad was sitting on a bench behind me, typing into his phone. I handed him mine.

'She wants to speak to you,' I said.

He listened to her shouting for a bit and then he said, 'He already knows.'

He said it in a dull voice, as if what I already knew was something everyday, as if what I already knew was Cindy was cooking cordon bleu for supper that night. He listened some more and then he said: 'I told you, Séverine, he already knows. He came back and found the removal men. He knows.'

He stood up and turned away from me; he walked towards the stone balustrade, over by the statues of the queens. I looked around. There was no one about. Soon we would be back at school and the jardin would fill up; there would be babysitters sitting in the shade by the sandpit, there would be kids playing football on the tarmac dalle, there would be new shoes, new backpacks, a fresh start. The sun beat down on my forehead. There was a cool green breeze about my feet. The dust hovering above the ground was bleached white: I could taste it in my mouth. I was so parched. Was it me? Was I why they broke up?

'It wasn't the way I would have chosen to tell him,' he said, talking to her patiently, as if she were a child. Then I don't know what she said, but he lost it as well and he started shouting back.

'You could have picked up the phone, Séverine, you could have read your texts. Where were you? At the hairdresser? At the Flore? Where the fuck were you?'

I kept my eyes closed until there was no more shouting. When I opened them, my dad was walking towards me, panting like he'd just got back from a run.

'*Voilà*,' he said, thrusting the phone into my hand. 'You see now why we're splitting up?'

He said it as if I'd tried to stop them, as if I had tried to tell him he couldn't do it. I knew then it was my only chance to stop it from happening, that moment in the jardin while he was still burning with anger, before it was set in stone, I could have saved their marriage if only I had the words. But I couldn't think of what to say that would make it better.

The day after that was Sunday and maman stayed in her bedroom. Cindy left for church and soon after the buzzer went. I pressed on the intercom and opened the door. My grandmother walked in, not my dad's mother, the other one.

'Hello, you,' she said. 'It's been an age since I saw you.'

She pulled her monogrammed wheelie trolley past me and parked it with a flourish in the salon. Her hair was darker than usual. She looked disappointed, the way she always looked.

'Where's your mother?' she said.

I wondered if my grandmother knew, if that was why she was here, to find out what was happening. She didn't come around that much; she lived in the 15ème arrondissement in the south-west of Paris with her son. She used to live with my grandfather in a suburb called Buzenval until my mother persuaded them to move to Paris. Maman hates the suburbs; she hates anything that is outside Paris, which is strange because she spent her whole childhood in Buzenval. 'You're Parisian by conquest, not birth, Séverine,' that's what my father used to say. Maman hated it when he said that.

My grandparents lived for only a year in the 15ème and then my grandfather's company sent him on a course advising people on how to retire without getting depressed. He ran off with the teacher of the course. Maude was her name. My grandparents had been married for thirty-seven years when he did that.

Now he lives with Maude in Malmaison. It's another suburb, next to Buzenval, where Napoléon and Joséphine had their country house. My grandparents took me to

Napoléon and Joséphine's château when I was little, before Maude. There were yellow roses in the garden and we ate strawberry tart that my grandfather bought at the bakery nearby. The strawberries were huge and covered in this sweet red syrup and there was a custardy cream underneath them and I let the cream and the red syrup and the pastry run up and down between my gums and the flesh of my inside cheek until it was warm and liquefied and then I got stung on the neck by a wasp and we had to go home.

After my grandfather left her, my grandmother drove out to Malmaison one Sunday morning, not to Joséphine's house, but to Maude's. She parked her car in Maude's drive and got out and punched her fist through the glass of a ground-floor window of Maude's house.

'*Pute de Malmaison, pute de Malmaison*,' whore of Malmaison, whore of Malmaison, she shouted. She kept shouting until the police came and got her. They took her to hospital; they had to give her an injection to stop her shouting. She needed eighteen stitches in her wrist. It's kind of funny now, although I don't see my grandfather any more.

'So, how was Dinard?' my grandmother asked me.

'OK.' I shrugged. 'Where are you going with the wheelie trolley?'

'I'm not going anywhere. I've come to stay with you.'

'With me?'

'Your mother needs me.'

I knew things must be bad if maman needed her.

She stayed all that week, buying the stationery for my new school, cooking the meals, telling Cindy what to do while maman lay in bed. I started senior school on Tuesday. I didn't hear from my father.

After a week in bed, maman got up and went to see a doctor, who gave her pills, helium pills, she called them. She said they made her feel like she was a balloon up on the ceiling looking down at us all and she quite liked that. The day after she started taking the pills, she went back to work. She said she had to go to the office because she owned the business and they couldn't cope without her. In the evening she came home and went to bed.

That was the beginning of her not going out. Before, she and my dad went out all the time. They went to dinners, openings, the cinema, Paris Photo, parties, cocktails; sometimes they went to three places in one night. But she didn't do that any more; she just hung around her bedroom in her leggings and a T-shirt. Her cheeks sunk and she looked sad.

On Saturday she didn't go out for brunch like she usually did, she didn't go shopping, she didn't go and get her hair done. Her personal trainer didn't come round. She just stayed in her bedroom all day. I went in to see her about 5 p.m. in the afternoon.

'Paul, come and watch with me,' she said and she patted the bed beside her. She'd sent her assistant out to Fnac to buy a box set of an American television series. We watched them one by one. She said it was good for my English. Sometimes I didn't get the jokes even with subtitles, I was eleven then, but I laughed when maman laughed. Her face went soft when she laughed, even though she was sad still.

She let me stay in their bed all afternoon with my back resting against the suede headboard and my legs tucked up under the duvet. My grandmother had gone home by then, so maman and I ordered pizza and we ate it in bed. She let me have the cheesy base and dough balls as well. They were hot and buttery in my mouth and I drank Coke cold from the can. After, we ate cookie-dough ice cream straight from the carton.

Around ten o'clock at night she said, 'I'm so tired, Paul. I've got to sleep.' She took her sleeping pill and then she switched off the bedside light. I sat in their bed and waited for her to say, 'Go to bed now, Paul, it's late,' but she didn't say that.

She fell asleep almost straightaway. I stayed watching the episode that was on, sitting in darkness with just the TV screen for light. It was past eleven when it finished. I heard a motorbike go by, then a voice shout out on the street below and then nothing. It was warm in the room, but I didn't want to get up and open a window. I had sweat on my back. I heard her breath go in and out; I watched her chest rise and fall. She was sad even in her sleep. I didn't want to get up and pee in case I woke her and it ended. I slipped down onto one shoulder so that my head was resting on the pillow; it was my father's pillow. I waited a bit and then I moved down some more, stretching my legs down along the mattress taking care not to kick her. I lay on my side looking away from her so that my breathing wouldn't wake her. My bladder felt half full, but I didn't dare get out of bed.

In the morning I woke up. I was facing my mother's back, lying on my side. Maman was still asleep. I lay and watched her. Her hair stretched over onto my father's pillow. I reached out and stroked it with just two fingers. After a while she woke up and turned. She saw me looking at her. She was beautiful in her half-sleep. Her lips were parted.

'*Coucou, toi*,' she said. '*Coucou, mon prince.*'

After that I slept in their bed every night. We never said anything about it, maman and I. I didn't ask if I could sleep there and she didn't say I could, I just did. I really loved that time. Strange, I know, to say I really loved it when my father left. But I did. Him not being there didn't change that much anyway because he'd never been there before. He left early for work; he worked late at night; they went out to dinner. At the weekend he was on his phone or out training or back in the office on a deal. What changed was that maman was there.

She would come back from the office around eight o'clock, I could hear her as she walked through the door, talking on the phone in the corridor, chatting to Estelle or her assistant, and then she would say, 'Listen, *ma belle*, I have to go, I've got my boy waiting for me.' She called me her boy, like I was her man now. Then she would see me and say, 'How was your day?' and she would stroke my hair as I told her how I hated school.

It felt right to share her bed at night; it felt as if that was where I should have been all my life, next to my mother. I don't mean replacing my father; I wouldn't have minded if he'd been there too, but he'd never let me stay in their bed. When I was little, if I had a nightmare or if I woke up cold because the duvet had fallen off the bed, I would go to their bedroom and I would stand by their bed waiting for maman to wake up. I would ask to get in, but my father always woke up then. '*Allez*, Paul,' he would say, 'you've got your own bed to go to.' I don't think he let me sleep in their bed once.

After he left I lay in their bed at night and watched maman as she took off her clothes. She looked at her naked body in the mirror. 'At least I've lost weight, Paul,' she said as she turned to see herself from behind, 'there's that to be said for all this.'

Then she would go into their bathroom to take her bath. I'd lie in bed and wait. When she came out I watched as she dried her body with a towel and rubbed her creams into her thighs, her legs, her breasts. While the cream sank into her skin, she walked around the room, pointing the remote control at the TV to turn it on. She must have known I was watching, but she never told me to stop. I watched as she put on her slip, holding her arms up, letting the satin cover her face, her breasts, before it slid in a waterfall over her body. The satin was the colour of nougat with raspberry lace at her breasts. She came and lay down in bed beside me. Her phone flashed with texts and messages, but she said to it: 'You can wait.'

She took her sleeping pill and then she switched off the bedside light and stroked my head in the dark. She touched my hair. I held her hand against my cheek and smelled the inside of her wrist, felt the pulse of her on my lips. I was happy then.

5

Maman was jogging down the hotel corridor, Cindy was running to keep up, pushing the pram with Lou, who was screaming and punching the air, writhing around on her sheepskin rug.

'Come on, Paul, I'm going to be late,' maman called out.

Every time I touched a door handle or a lift button in that hotel I got a massive electric shock. It must have been my trainers. I had taken to slamming the handles and buttons with my hand to lessen the shock of the charge. If I ran now I'd give off sparks.

We pushed to get in the lift. It was packed with people going to the thalasso, all trying to look cool about the fact they were in a lift wearing white towelling dressing gowns and white plastic slippers. There was no room for the pram.

'You'll have to wait for the next one,' maman said to Cindy as the doors sucked shut.

I wondered if Cindy ever felt like shouting, ever felt like shoving her foot in the door and saying, 'Move your arse, I'm coming in.' But she never does that; she just smiles, or if she doesn't exactly smile, then she looks blank, she accepts. I've never seen her angry. Once I saw her upset when her grandmother died and she couldn't go home to the funeral because she's got no papers. Then she went quiet for days. But otherwise she is always smiling and nodding.

She reads the Bible every night and she has posters in her room that say things like 'God makes all things bright and beautiful' with pictures of daisies and sunsets. She's got a poster of Jesus holding a child and saying: 'Let the little children come to me,' and his hair is gold and his beard is gold and he's wearing a white gown like he's just stepped off a cloud. My aunt Catherine has a painting of Jesus in her apartment, but her Jesus is wearing a crown of thorns shoved down on his scalp and he's got blood dripping down his temples, and his face is battered and green.

People pushed to get out when the lift doors opened, and then they ran across the foyer like it was the first day of the sales. There were two large rooms for breakfast, one with the food and the other with the tables. The waiter showed maman straight to a table; she didn't bother with the food. I went to check out the buffet. Scarlett was standing in the queue. She was right in front of me, so near I could touch her. She was putting chocolate-chip cookies onto her plate, loading them up, three or four of them alongside slices of dark red salami. She turned and looked at me. Her eyes were yellow-green with a dark circle around the iris, as if someone had drawn it in. I'd never been that close to her.

'Are you doing club ado, you?' she said.

'No,' I said. 'Are you?'

'I'm not doing that shit. I'm fourteen.'

I wondered if she recognized me from school.

'Who are you here with?' she asked.

'My mother.'

'Which one is she?'

'She's over there, in black, by the window.'

She looked across to where maman was sitting. She checked her out. Then she turned back to me.

'She's beautiful,' she said. 'And she knows it.'

I waited for her to say something else, the sort of thing people usually say, like why is she so thin and you're so fat or you don't look anything like her, why is that? But she didn't say that. She tossed back her hair and looked around at the tables of towelling people.

'Fucking thalasso,' she said. 'People paying money to get their cellulite hosed down with a cold power jet, what a joke. Remind me not to grow old.'

She wore strands of coloured embroidery on her right wrist and a little black ribbon with a silver heart on it. Her arms were tanned and thin and she had scraps of dark purple polish on her fingernails. Her eyebrows were thick and black and arched like a woman's, but beneath them she had the face of a girl.

She popped a gherkin in her mouth.

'See you later,' she said. She went and sat at the table where her parents were reading the newspaper.

'So what are you going to do today?' maman asked as I sat down. She looked at my plate, counted the number of chouquette pastries there, but she didn't say anything. 'Are you sure you don't want to do club ado?'

'I told you, I'm not doing that.'

'What are you going to do all day? I'm putting Lou in baby club. Cindy, you need to come with me now to drop Lou off, then you need to pick her up at five o'clock because I don't finish until five-thirty. Have you understood that, Cindy?'

'Yes, madam, I've understood.' Cindy was feeding Lou a bottle. Maman got out a plastic folder with a cream card inside it.

'What is that?' I asked.

'It's my schedule,' she said. 'They've put me down for aqua-gym straight after balneotherapy. I'll never get there. Why do they make it so stressful?'

People started to get up from the tables, pushing back their chairs, checking their phones, standing up and draining their coffee, telling their kids to hurry, to leave the hot chocolate, there wasn't time. It was just like Megève or the hotel in St-Barth where we used to go: guys on their phones, women trying to get to their spa treatments, rushing out of the room to dump their children at kids' club. Piou Piou, club fun, club ado; the names are different, but it's all the same, you pay your money and they take your kids away.

'So what are you gonna do, Paul?' maman said again. She stood up and smoothed her black Lycra leggings against her thighs. I saw the waiter go by and check out her arse.

I shrugged. 'Hang out.'

'Are you sure?' She looked at her watch and then she pulled fifty euros from her purse and passed them to me. 'I won't be back until five-thirty. I guess Gabriel can look after you when he gets here.'

I rolled my eyes.

'He can't even look after himself,' I said.

But she wasn't listening. She was giving Cindy instructions about feeds, talking about milk millilitres and droplets of medicine and Lou stuff. Everyone was trying to get out of the dining room at the same time, man, you could feel the tension, flapping their schedules, trainers grating on the carpet, all the Lycra and towelling and plastic slippers generating kilowatts of electrical charge. Then maman was gone, and Cindy and the pram were jogging after her.

I did a last tour of the buffet table. I picked up a pain au chocolat, a maple-syrup twist, and another handful of chouquettes. They are puffballs of choux pastry rolled in crystallized white sugar. I lick the pearls of sugar off first, then, when the choux pastry is wet and shiny, I pop it in my mouth and hold it there until the puffball collapses and turns to pulp.

I walked through to the bar and sat down on one of the big purple sofas. The coffee table in front of me had legs carved to look like huge lion paws with black claws sticking out. I watched the receptionists through a glass wall. Gwénaëlle was there, the receptionist who had checked us in. She was sitting on a stool, chatting to her colleague. She had taken off her shoes and I could see her beige stockings; I watched as she rubbed one foot up against her slim calf, like a cat.

Serge from the night before came into the bar with a slimmer version of himself. They sat opposite me and drank espressos and talked about how much they'd lost at the casino the night before. I played FIFA.

I looked up just as Scarlett walked through the hotel door. She was carrying a plastic shopping bag from 8 à Huit.

'What a hole,' she said as she sat down beside me on the sofa. She was wearing white frayed jean shorts even though it was cold out and she'd left the button undone so they were open on her tanned stomach. I looked down and I could see the top of her yellow knickers. Serge looked up and stared at her.

'I just walked into town. There is nothing there, just a bunch of bourgeois women buying roast chicken.'

I laughed, but I didn't say anything. I couldn't think of what to say. She got her phone out.

'What the fuck is that about?' She pointed at a black shiny sculpture of a huge woman in a tiny bikini with her legs in the air. 'That is sick,' she said. She took a photo of the sculpture. She didn't seem to need me to say anything. She looked around; she checked out Serge. She took a photo of us both on her phone and sent it to someone. That person must have sent something back because she started laughing. She was like that for a long time, texting and messaging, giggling to herself, while I sat beside her on the warm velvet sofa, gaming. It was a nice feeling.

'Where are your parents?' I asked after a bit.

'Golf and thalassotherapy.' She shrugged. 'As usual.' And then she said, 'Let's go down to the beach.'

We walked past the outdoor pool where kids were having swimming lessons. There was lounge music being piped out of the bamboo. We went out to the promenade, where there were still some stragglers heading off to the thalasso. They looked odd walking along the road dressed in white dressing gowns.

'It's like a psychiatric ward,' Scarlett said.

'Have you been?'

'Have I been where?' she said.

'To the thalasso.'

'Yeah, I've been. My mum spends half her life in there. Here and in Quiberon. Quiberon's not so bad because it's got a hot tub outside. That's cool.'

We walked past the glass dome of the thalasso; people were heading in there like bees to a hive.

'What do they do all day?' I asked.

'Nothing. That's the point. They scrub you down with salt, they smother you with green seaweed that smells rank, and then they wrap you up in this plastic sheet and plug it in so you deep-fat-fry and sweat into the plastic. Then they get you out and hose you down with cold water and you have a bath with all these purple twinkly lights and they tell you all this crap about the benefits of seawater and how you are going to live for twenty-four thousand years. Then you spend hours lying around in there.' She pointed to the side of the building. 'It's got special glass so they can see us, but we can't see them.'

'What do they do in there?'

'Nothing. My mum's probably in there right now.'

She stuck out her tongue at the glass building. 'Yeah, that is the worst in there, you just lie around "resting" and everyone reads *Gala* magazine and stares at each other to see who's had bad plastic surgery. Then at the end of the week, they weigh you and tell you how much less stressed you feel. The joke of it is my mum never loses more than half a kilo, max.'

'How do you know all that?'

'I've been so many times and I watch people. Like you do,' she said, and she looked straight at me.

'My mum's doing the "young mother" treatment,' I said.

'Yeah, well, my mum can't do that, can she? She's not young and she hasn't got a baby. She's doing the anti-stress treatment. She's got loads of that. Don't I know it?'

I wondered if maman still counted as a young mother. She would be forty next year. I guess she did have a baby.

We walked down the steps onto the sand. The beach was flat and it went on for ever. The sun had come out after yesterday's rain and there were runners out in shorts and kids from the hotel kids' club being made to do a high-jump competition. There were masses of tiny white shells all over the sand. They crunched under our shoes as we walked. The sea was far out. It was odd; it wasn't like a normal beach. There were no waves; there was no rush of the sea, no excitement, just these flat lines. It felt like a runway to somewhere.

We sat down together about half-way between the promenade and the sea. I dragged my fingers around like I was a digger, making little piles of the cold, clammy sand. Seven piles on each side of my body, small and round, each the same size.

'Where's your dad?' Scarlett said.

'At work, I guess. They're not together.'

'And the baby?'

'She's not my dad's.'

'What's she called?'

'Lou,' I said.

'It must be nice to have a baby sister.' Her voice was different when she said that. Not hard and diamond-cut, but tender.

'She's only my half-sister,' I said. 'She doesn't actually do anything.'

'She will when she's older. She'll want to play with you then. She'll hold your hand, she'll look up to you. You'll be her big brother.' She pulled out a half-bottle of vodka from her shopping bag.

'What about you? Have you got brothers and sisters?' I asked.

'An older brother.' She took a swig of vodka and offered me the bottle. I took a swig. I'd never drunk vodka before. I would have preferred Coke. 'But he's a total geek,' she said, 'a mathmo. He's doing his prépas.' She looked across at me to see if I understood the significance of what she was saying. Prépas meant he was doing a course to try to get into one of the grandes écoles, which are the best universities in France. It meant he was clever. It takes two years to do it, you work like crazy and then at the end you take an exam that is a competition, and only the top scorers get accepted for a grande école.

'My dad did that,' I said, 'and my uncle too.' That is what my cousin Augustin would do after his Bac next year. That is what my dad used to dream I would do.

'We used to hang out when we were little,' she said. 'But then he got all serious when he went to senior school. He became a Scout, you know, carrying the flag with the cross and singing Jesus songs. All he wanted to do was run around in his Scout uniform or study. Nothing else. He didn't need me any more.'

I saw her looking at me out of the corner of her eye, to see my reaction, I guess. I kept making my mounds of sand. She told me the name of the school where he was doing his prépas. It was the big Catholic school near us where the girl with black hair who lives opposite us goes. I'd had swimming lessons there when I was little. All the boys have to wear shirts with collars and have their hair cut above their ears, and the girls aren't allowed to wear short skirts or make up. Everyone says it's so strict you get detention if you drop your ruler.

'I used to go to that school,' Scarlett said.

I laughed out loud.

'What are you laughing at?' she said.

I stopped laughing.

'What, you think I'm not clever enough to go there, is that it?' She made her eyes go narrow.

'No, it's not that. I can't imagine you there, that's all.'

'Yeah, well, I got chucked out,' she said.

'What for?'

'Bad attitude.' She took a swig of vodka. 'Big, bad attitude, that's what they said. I'd been there since I was five. I just couldn't take it any more. Everywhere was dark and everyone was strict and trussed up, telling me there was something wrong with me, that I lacked discipline. And all the kids looked at me like they were scared of me. The priests and the teachers there, they all go on about Christ's suffering. They don't know what suffering is.' Her mouth was tight when she said that.

She took her jean jacket off and I could see her breasts, pushed up and out for all to see. She kept jutting them out, as if they would reach the sea. She was wearing a lip-gloss that glistened pink and after she took off her jacket, I could smell the sweetness of her perfume. The boys at school talked about her breasts all the time; it was strange to think I was sitting here next to them. I wondered if she would let me touch them if I reached out my hand. I wondered what Guillaume and Pierre would say if they knew I was here, sitting next to Scarlett Lacasse on the beach in La Baule.

She got up then and threw the bottle to the ground.

'Chase me!' she shouted.

She ran all the way down the beach and I chased after

her; she ran and ran and I ran after her down to the sea. She kicked off her black ballerinas so they flew through the air, then she ripped off her shorts and I could see all of her lacy yellow knickers and she went and paddled in the still sea. I took my shoes and socks off, but not my jeans. I rolled them up to my knees. I followed her into the sea. The water was freezing cold and green and it made my toes look yellow. Scarlett waded out really far, but still the water was only up to her thighs.

She went on and on, moving further away from me. I stayed at the edge with just my feet and ankles submerged. Little silver fish darted across my toes. She looked like she was in a film, wading all alone in the sea with the wintry sun on her hair. Her head was down, like she was searching for something in the water. I watched her because I couldn't take my eyes off her. I didn't want to let Scarlett out of my sight, out of my life, now that she was here.

6

After a while she came wading back to where I was waiting.

'I hate it when there are no waves.' She was like a little girl when she said that. She put her shorts back on and picked up her ballerinas.

'Have you got any money?' she said.

'I've got fifty euros.'

'What are we waiting for?'

We walked back up the beach past some old guys digging in the sand for razor clams. They had narrow forks and buckets and I heard one of them shout: 'I've got him now, Claude.' We found a cafe tucked under the wall on the beach, just below the promenade. It was called Club de l'Étoile. It was warm inside; the floor was orange and the chairs were yellow plastic and there was some kind of Cuban music playing and little coloured lights strung up above the bar. I loved that place. There was sand between the floorboards and starfish everywhere, dried starfish and little blue fake starfish on the tables and starfish shapes cut out of the wooden bar. The lady brought us cheeseburgers and fries with ketchup. We drank Coke. Scarlett told me her mum would be angry with her for ever for getting chucked out of school.

'What about your dad?' I asked.

'What about him?' She took a massive slurp of Coke through a pink straw.

'What does he say?'

'He says, "Scarlett, there is no mystery to life. You work hard and you succeed. You muck around and you fail. And then you fail for life."' She ate a fry. 'Only César loves me,' she said.

'Who's César?'

'He's my dog, only he's more than a dog, he's super-intelligent and he knows all my feelings, all my secrets. He understands me.' She pulled out her phone and showed me about forty photos of César. He was a really hairy golden retriever, pale cream with sad black eyes and a black nose. She showed me photos of them lying together on a sheepskin rug. Just looking at him made me feel asthmatic.

'He's my baby,' she said in a girlish voice. 'César loves his mummy.' A message came in on her phone. She said it was from Stéphane and that they'd been going out for six weeks now. 'He's OK,' she said, 'but he's super-arrogant.' She messaged him back. 'He's on holiday in Dubai and he keeps telling me all the girls are really hot, trying to make me jealous.'

Her eyelashes were thick with black mascara, and a little ball of it had collected in the corner of her left eye. She had loads of dangly Japanese things on her phone and she played with them all the time. She couldn't keep her fingers off her phone, scrolling, scrolling, scrolling.

She kept putting the phone down on the table, flicking her hair and then checking the phone again straightaway to see if anyone had texted or messaged her.

We ate fries for a bit without saying anything. They'd gone cold, but the salt made them good. She held up her phone and used it as a mirror; she looked at herself for a long time, but I wasn't sure she was happy with what she saw. She wiped away the clog-ball of mascara; she put on some lip-gloss.

Then she said, 'What about you?'

'What about me?'

'Your parents, what are they like? You know, do they put you under pressure?'

'They used to, when I was in junior school.' I told her how they wanted me to go to the school where Estelle's son goes. It was easy talking to Scarlett; it was like she understood. So I told her everything. I told her that's why we bought an apartment near the Jardin du Luxembourg in the first place, to be near the school I didn't get into. I told her I tried three times to get in. I told her about the tutoring twice a week and my parents organizing dinners to try to get me accepted.

'They were obsessed, that's all they ever talked about, the application, the exam, the interview, who else was taking the exam, who else was waiting to hear. I remember when we got the letter from the school, maman ripped it open and her face went white. "Oh my god, Paul. It can't be true." Then she rang my dad and she shouted down the phone at him: "He wasn't taken. Do you hear me? He wasn't taken. What are we going to do? What the hell are we going to do?"'

I looked up. Scarlett was watching me, waiting. So I went on.

'My dad called the school, he sent emails, he called his friends, he got them to call the school, he tried all this pressure, but they just kept saying no, there was no place for me. After that, it was like someone had died. They walked around without speaking or I'd come into a room and they would stop talking. Sometimes maman would call Estelle and I couldn't hear the conversation, but I knew what she was saying. My dad could hardly bring himself to speak to me. Maman has her own production business and she puts together advertising shoots with models and photographers and hundreds of people in Tokyo and Milan, places like that, and my dad does one-billion-euro deals and he earns loads. I guess they couldn't believe they couldn't get their son into the school they wanted him to go to. Either that or they couldn't believe I couldn't get myself into the school they wanted me to go to. They just couldn't handle it. It was like me being a failure made them a failure too.'

'I get that all the time,' Scarlett said. 'Like you are letting them down because you're not the big success they think they are. My parents spend their life saying, "I despair of you. You need to work harder. Success comes only through striving. Look at Jean-Benoît, look how hard he works to succeed."'

'Who's Jean-Benoît?' I said.

Her face sucked in like a sea anemone does when you touch it.

'My brother,' she said.

I wondered how it was that she was called Scarlett, which is the kind of name a singer in a band or a waitress at the Hôtel Costes has, and her brother had a super-classic French name. I wanted to ask her, but I didn't dare; she looked as if she'd smack me one if I said the wrong thing.

'I changed my name,' she said, 'if that's what you are thinking.'

'That's cool.' I took a slurp of Coke so I didn't have to say anything.

'Not like officially, on paper and stuff. I just did it when I got chucked out of school. I'd had enough and I wanted to be free. Free from that shit.'

'What did your parents do when you changed it?'

'They think it's ridiculous and they refuse to call me Scarlett. But they can't do anything about it. When I started at our school they gave me papers to fill in and there's a bit where you put the name you want to be known by. It's supposed to be for people who want to be called by their middle names, but I put down Scarlett, and the admin woman, Madame Lebrun, said that was OK.'

'She's nice,' I said.

'Yeah, she's one of the reasons I like our school.'

I wanted to ask Scarlett what her real name was, but her face was still sucked in.

'Victoire,' she said, 'and if you tell anyone at school, I'll break your legs.'

'I like Victoire,' I said.

'I don't,' she said.

She was on her phone forever after that. I ordered tiramisu. I gamed a bit. I ate my dessert. The waitress came over and gave us the bill in a little metal pot, then later she came back again and said she wanted to settle up because she was finishing her shift, so I paid for the Cokes and the burgers and fries and the tiramisu. The waitress gave us each a strawberry-flavoured Chupa Chupp lolly. The wrappers were faded and stuck to the lollipop; they must have been left over from the summer.

We went back out on the beach. The afternoon light was draining out of the sky. The kids' club kids had gone in. There were seagulls standing on one leg in pools of water, looking out to sea.

'Why did your parents break up?' she asked.

'I don't know,' I said. 'I wish I knew, but I don't.'

'Probably an affair, most people in the 6ème break up because of affairs. Most people in Paris break up because of affairs.'

'How do you know that?'

'I watched a TV programme about it – you know, one of those programmes where real people tell you about their affairs and what went wrong and how they got found out. They said if couples break up it's normally not just one affair, it's lots of them. But, I mean, everyone is doing it, so I don't see why it's such a big deal. But I guess if everyone is doing it, that's why everyone is breaking up.'

'I don't know if it was an affair,' I said. 'I don't know what it was. My dad is massively into training, you know, triathlons and stuff.'

'Ah, yeah,' she said and she looked excited about that. 'That is classic, that is, the guy goes nuts about training and his body. He spends so long training and obsessing about his abs that he forgets he has a wife.'

'How do you know that?'

'I read about it in *Elle*. I'm always reading about relationships. I want to be a psychologist when I'm older.'

I thought she could help me. I mean, she seemed to know so much about divorce that maybe she could help me figure it out.

'But my mum's obsessed with her body too,' I said. 'So I don't see why she would have minded him being obsessed with his body. She's always working out, Pilates and kickboxing, she has a personal trainer who comes to the house three times a week, she does all this detox fasting, you know, and she does all these injections.'

'Botox?'

'Yeah, she does that, but she does some new thing as well, some kind of vitamin acid that they stick in your cheeks to make them look like apples. She does it when she goes to New York. It's some French guy who lives in New York.'

'Oh my god,' Scarlett said and her eyes were open wide. 'I know about him, I read about him. I can't believe your mum goes to him – she really goes to him?'

'Yeah,' I said, 'she really does.'

'Respect,' she said.

'So what I mean is, it wasn't just one of them and not the other getting obsessed. They are both obsessed with their bodies. My dad does it for fitness, to be hard and win, and my mum does it to be beautiful, to be thin and win. And I think they liked being beautiful together, winning by their beauty.'

Terriblement beau. That's what the guy who used to look after the plants on the balcony said about my parents once. He said it with a funny look on his face, so I wasn't sure it was a compliment. He had long grey hair; he was a bit of a hippie and he was always smoking pot out on the balcony as he watered the plants.

'Maybe they got off on the fact the other was beautiful,' Scarlett said.

'Yeah, they definitely did. They met on a plane coming back from New York, sitting next to each other in business class. My dad used to say it was love at first sight.'

We stood for a bit saying nothing, both of us looking out to sea, and then I said:

'You know what I think? I think I am why they broke up. I mean, I didn't get into the school they wanted me to go to. That was in May and three months later they broke up.'

'They are not going to break up over your school.'

'You don't know my parents. Maman was obsessed with that school, all she wanted was for me to go there so she could tell all her friends and go for coffee with the other cool mums. And my dad just wanted me to be a winner. He wanted to tell his parents, to tell his brother. It's not just that I didn't get into the school, it's maths – I'm bad at maths and I can't play good tennis and my dad loves tennis. I am not what they wanted me to be. I don't live up to them.'

I remembered that final Sunday lunch when they fought about the macaroons all the way to my grand-parents' house, and when we finally got there, my dad parked the car and I opened the car door and there was a welt of mauve petrol on the tarmac right by my feet. I didn't want to step in the petrol in my brand-new trainers, so I took my time getting out of the car to avoid it.

'For god's sake, hurry up, will you?' my dad had said. Something about his voice made me look up. I looked straight into his eyes. There was hate there, hate for me. He turned away, but I had seen it.

'You know what?' Scarlett said. 'Fucking parents, it's all about them, their hang-ups. Your dad is worried you can't play tennis because he's worried it makes him look bad. That's his problem. You're his child, not his car. He can get over it. He can go and run another fucking marathon. You're not here to make him look good. *Allez*, Paul.' She grabbed my arm and she ran holding my hand, dragging me with her, down to the swings. When we got there, there were two little kids playing on them. Scarlett told them to get lost and they jumped off without a word. They ran crying back up the beach to find their parents. Scarlett took the yellow swing and I took the red and we swung back and forth, back and forth. She could go really high; she kept kicking her legs out and snatching them back and she got higher and higher.

'Watch me,' she said, 'watch how I do it.'

And so I watched her and after a while I started going higher and she kept laughing and shouting.

'*Encore*, Paul, more, more, more.'

And I started laughing too, because it was funny to be doing this, to be swinging high on the beach in La Baule in October. I had never done this before; I had never felt this freedom.

As she got lower, she shouted out, 'I'm gonna jump.' She waited until the swing was coming through and she jumped far out so the swing wouldn't hit her, far, far out and she landed on her feet and then she fell forward into the sand and she lay there laughing and writhing. Then she turned to me and, lying on her back, she shouted: 'Do it, Paul.'

'I can't,' I said. 'I can't do it.'

'Do it,' she said again. 'Do it. Wait till I say go.'

I swung back up and I looked out at the sea and I shouted, 'I am here. I am here.' I don't know why I shouted that and then I went down and then I went up again and as I came down, Scarlett shouted, 'Now, Paul, now.' And I flew forwards through the air. 'Jump,' she was shouting. '*Vas-y*, jump, do it, do it, do it.' I remember that jump.

I'd never felt like that before, like my mouth was flying through the air, like I was free and Scarlett was flying with me. I felt this lightness that was Scarlett and me. Scarlett and me. Scarlett and me. Scarlett and me.

My feet landed and planted and I fell forward and got dumped into the damp sand. It didn't hurt. I laughed out loud.

'Too good,' I said, 'it was too good.'

She lay down beside me and we laughed. We laughed and lay on our backs and we held hands as we kept laughing.

'Your face,' she said, 'your face, it was too funny to see your face.'

We watched as all the blues on the horizon and the white of the clouds merged into a band of steel grey and we lay together in the cold sand.

After a while she got a message on her phone.

'*Merde*,' she said. 'I have to go.'

My jeans were wet and my back was cold when I stood up. We brushed off the damp sand.

'I've left my bag up there with all my stuff. Come with me?'

She ran on ahead and I jogged behind her. It took us a while to find where she'd left her stuff. She picked up the vodka and took a big gulp of it, then she looked inside the plastic bag and pulled out a small bright blue and silver breath freshener and she sprayed it three times into her mouth.

'They'll never know,' she said and she smiled at me.

People were leaving the thalasso. It was the end of the day. We watched the line of towelling-white bodies file along the promenade back towards the hotel and then I saw a red glow bobbing towards us; it was the burning tip of a cigar. I put my hand on Scarlett's arm.

'Wait,' I said. We stopped. We were at the bottom of the steps that led up to the promenade. Gabriel was jogging towards us, not jogging for exercise, but jogging because he was late. He had his jeans on and his leather jacket and every so often his cigar flared red and then faded.

'What is it?' she said.

'It's him.'

'Who?'

'My mother's boyfriend.'

'What's he like?'

'He's an arsehole.'

Gabriel looked down at where we stood as if he'd just heard what I said.

'Hey, Paul,' he shouted. 'What's up?'

He stopped jogging and walked to the edge of the promenade so that he was standing above us.

'Aren't you going to introduce me to your friend, Paul?' he said.

'Scarlett, this is Gabriel,' I said.

'Hey, Scarlett,' he said.

We walked slowly up the steps towards him.

'Great name you have, very rock'n'roll.'

Scarlett said nothing; she just stared up at him.

'So, what have you guys been up to? You look a little damp, like you've been rolling around in the sand.' He smiled suggestively as he said that.

'Hanging out,' I said.

'Well, while you've been hanging out, I just won myself a quick three hundred and forty euros at the casino, just like that.' He snapped his fingers. His lips were stained dark red. 'Lady luck on my first day, how about that?'

'I've always wanted to go to the casino,' Scarlett said.

'I'll take you sometime.' Gabriel smiled at her.

'She's not old enough,' I said.

'Oh, I'm sure I could find a way to get her in.' He raised one eyebrow like he was James Bond. 'What do you say, Scarlett?'

'I'm going back to Paris tonight,' she said.

'Well, that's too bad, maybe next time.'

We headed back to the hotel and Gabriel talked non-stop about blackjack and how he'd won. Scarlett and I walked in silence. I didn't want her to go. She hadn't told me she was leaving. We turned into the back entrance of the hotel. The chandeliers were lit up in the lobby.

'It was cool hanging out,' she said to me.

'Yeah,' I said. I couldn't think of what else to say and Gabriel was standing right there listening to every word.

'See you at school, then,' she said.

'Yeah,' I said, 'see you at school.'

'Don't tell me you guys are at the same school,' Gabriel said, letting his mouth hang open. 'Man, you're too lucky to be young.'

Scarlett fixed him with her yellow-green eyes.

'How old are you?' she said.

He looked embarrassed.

'Thirty-five.'

She whistled through her teeth.

'You're pretty old. Not like dying-old, but, I mean, you're not young, are you?'

'Well, thanks,' Gabriel said. He looked sad then.

Scarlett leaned forward and kissed my cheeks.

'So long, Paul,' she said.

She walked away towards the lobby, swaying her butt as she went, knowing that we were watching her, then she disappeared behind the people and the potted palms and I couldn't see her any more.

Gabriel slapped my shoulder.

'Hey, I like your taste, Paul. Her style's a little destroy. She's cute though,' he said. 'I'm going up to take a shower before your mother gets home.'

I went and lay on a lounger by the pool. The cream canvas was damp beneath me where someone else had lain. I watched the steam rising up off the water. Someone had left a bowl of pretzels and nuts on the side table. The evening air had turned the pretzels soft, but I ate them anyway. And then I ate the nuts. I wished she hadn't told him she wanted to go to the casino. Why did he have to ruin everything by turning up? I covered myself in one of the pool towels to stay warm.

The light was fading all around me. The pool was lit up and the underwater lights made the water shimmer and the bodies inside the pool glow in the steam and the oncoming night.

A boy and a girl were screaming in the pool, a girl with a sexy tanned stomach and a white-fringed bikini chasing a guy around in the shallow end, fake fighting when all they really wanted to do was make out. You could hear it in their voices, in the girl's high-pitched screams. The white fringes of her bikini swayed with her every move. I closed my eyes and licked the last of the peanut salt from my lips. I listened to them splashing and squealing. I lay there with my eyes closed and imagined it was me in the pool, that it was me being chased around in the steam by Scarlett wearing only a white-fringed bikini.

My phone buzzed in my pocket. I got it out. There was a message from Scarlett.

'You're right,' she said, 'he's an arsehole.'

7

My dad came by the Sunday after we got back from La Baule to take me for lunch with my grandparents in Neuilly. He texted me to say he was downstairs. Maman and Gabriel were still in bed. I found Cindy in the kitchen bent over Lou, singing to her as she fed her a bottle.

'I'm going, Cindy,' I said. She gave a little start and Lou broke off from her bottle; she swivelled her eyes round to look at me. She had a froth of yellowish milk seeping out of the corner of her mouth. She didn't smile. I wondered if she even knew who I was. She looked in my direction for a couple of seconds with her mouth open and then she turned back to her bottle and sucked furiously, as if someone had tried to take it away. All the warm milk that she had guzzled since she was born had gone straight to her cheeks; they were bulging like a chipmunk's. She had a bald patch on the back of her head. Cindy told me it was where her head rubbed against the mattress. Cindy massaged it with almond oil every day to try to get the hair to grow back. I touched her head once when no one was looking; it was rough where the hair was matted and broken.

My dad was downstairs with the engine running.

He kissed me when I got in the car.

'How was La Baule?'

'Good,' I said.

'Did you play some tennis?'

'No.'

'Why not?'

'I didn't feel like it.'

'What about kids' club, did you do kids' club?' he turned onto the Rue d'Assas.

'Maman says I don't have to do that any more.'

We sat in silence. We drove past school.

'So what did you do?' he said.

'I hung out with a friend.'

He looked across at me when I said the word friend.

'Is she your girlfriend?'

'No,' I said.

His phone went then. He answered it and said:

'Yeah, I'm going to Neuilly. I'll be back later on. I'm with Paul. I'll text you when I'm leaving. Not late.'

'Who was that?' I asked as he put the phone down.

'A girl.'

'Who?'

'Irinka,' he said.

'What kind of name is that?'

'She's Russian.'

I imagined a girl in a movie, a Russian blonde who has sex with you, then shoots you with a silencer and leaves with the stolen encoder. Irinka. How come Irinka knew my name before I knew hers?

'Is she nice?' I said.

My dad made a shape with his lips, like he was tasting a first mouthful of soup.

'She's OK,' he said. 'She needs a lot of attention.' Then he smiled to himself. 'More than I can give.'

We headed out of Paris, going west. La Défense was a dark gateway on the horizon. We sat with all the other Sunday drivers on the Champs-Élysées, queuing to get through the lights, watching the tourists milling in and out of the shops. The traffic freed up after the Arc de Triomphe and my dad accelerated down the Avenue de la Grande Armée. The Porsche reared up and we burned past the rest of the cars. He allowed himself another smile then.

We drove fast through the Bois de Boulogne. It was misty and damp among the trees; the leaves were burned red and yellow and they fell onto the windscreen as we passed. I watched the people getting onto the little white train that takes you to the Jardin d'Acclimatation. It's a kind of permanent funfair in the middle of the woods and there are rides and a carousel with seats that hang from chains and fly up as it turns around. There are ponies too and sheep kept in a pen and a Guignol puppet show.

We used to go there after we had lunch at my grandparents' apartment, just maman and me. We would go as soon as lunch was over, before my grandmother had a chance to serve coffee. 'Quick, let's get out of here,' maman used to say as she rushed me out of my grandparents' apartment building. She kept her hand on the small of my back, pushing me forward, glancing over her shoulder as if they might be following.

I loved the electric-racehorse ride the most. I always chose the painted black horse with flared red nostrils. I would climb up and maman would sit behind me, holding me tight around the waist.

'Faster,' she would whisper in my ear, 'faster, Paul.'

But the black horse couldn't go any faster – all of the horses went at the same fixed speed – and I was glad, because it meant the ride lasted longer. We bobbed up and down between the trees and hedgerows, through long grasses and past little ponds. It was silent away from the crowds. I had maman all to myself.

I stared out at the big white machinery of the funfair rides. There was something sad about the Jardin d'Acclimatation, even back then when I was little; all those people with their kids in pushchairs trying to escape apartments, paying to go on rides, hoping they would last for ever. And there was the feeling that Sunday was already half-way over; I knew that school was tomorrow, I saw the grown-ups checking their watches, I heard maman sigh and say, 'We should go back.'

I wished someone had told me then it wouldn't last for ever. I pressed the button to lower the passenger window. I could smell the piss from the mangy sheep that were kept on the other side of the fencing. A bunch of Mylar helium balloons were caught up in a tree: a pink pony, a red metallic heart, and a silvery white unicorn, all swaying above the branches. And I thought, I am no longer a child.

A woman and her Irish setter went running by. She had her music player strapped around her bare arm and she was pounding along as fast as her dog. I thought of Scarlett and César. She told me they had a Portuguese housekeeper who looked after César. I wouldn't really want a dog like César because they leave hair everywhere. But she says she loves his silky hair. I hadn't seen Scarlett since La Baule. She'd messaged me, but we weren't yet back at school.

There were vans parked up all along the road doing Sunday-morning business in the grey mist. I knew what those women were waiting for, the ones standing around the back of the vans, that white woman with straight yellow hair wearing cut-off jean shorts and black thigh-high boots, flicking the rotten leaves off her heels. She looked a bit like Pierre's old babysitter from Romania. She was waiting for a car to stop. The tops of her thighs were purple and mottled. She stared into our car to see if we would slow. Her eyes were gaping like a dead fish's.

The other side of the Bois de Boulogne, near the Porte Dauphine, is where the transvestites hang out. I've seen them standing at the roundabout swinging their hand-bags. Brazilian boys; they wear hot-pants and fake eyelashes and they pace up and down the side of the road, hoisting their arses up against car windows, shouting, come and get it if you dare.

If you think about it, it's pretty funny all the sex that's for sale around here. This is where rich old people live, people like my grandparents and their friends, women who play bridge and wear Chanel, men who have the red silken threads of the Légion d'Honneur embroidered on their suit lapels. Every time they walk out of their apartments they see it: van doors open onto dirty mattresses, pimps counting money under the trees, women on benches plucking their eyebrows while they wait.

Once when I was in junior school, my grandmother and I were walking down the avenue where she lived and a black woman came out of the bushes. It was nine o'clock in the morning and she was naked except for these weird black straps pulled tight around her breasts and her arse. She stumbled as she came out of the undergrowth, catching her foot on a branch, and everything wobbled. A man was right behind her. He was a young white guy wearing a T-shirt and doing up his jeans. I remember he had his hand on his zip.

I pulled my grandmother's arm to get her attention.

'What's she doing?' I said.

The woman was right there in front of us, about five metres away. I could see the sweat on her upper lip. I could see the marks where the leather straps bit into her flesh.

'Who?' my grandmother said.

'That woman, right there.' I pointed at her, tried to make my grandmother see.

But she just kept her eyes straight ahead.

'She must be looking for her dog,' she said and she grabbed my wrist – she held me so tightly I had red marks after – and we started to cross the road right there, even though there were no traffic lights to get across. She put her hand up, commanding the traffic to stop, and then she pulled me out in front of the cars.

They were all there in the salon, my grandparents, my aunt and uncle, my cousins. They were waiting for me and my dad when we walked in. They rose as one.

'We thought you'd never come,' my grandfather said.

There were red and cream flowers in a pot on the shiny black grand piano. My grandmother was wearing a red skirt and a cream blouse as if she'd dressed to match her flowers. She had large pearl earrings and a strand of pearls around her neck. Her hair was a shimmering blond puff. 'The blow-dry from hell', maman used to call it. My grandmother gets up early to look like that.

'How are you, my little Paul?' She leaned forward to kiss me.

My grandfather's silver hair was brushed smooth. His face was tanned from their holiday in Vietnam and he was wearing his pale blue cashmere V-neck that made his winter tan stand out even more. He smelled of lemons.

'Now that you are here, Philippe, we can celebrate,' he said to my father.

'What are we celebrating?' my father said as he kissed my aunt Catherine hello.

'We have your brother's promotion to celebrate.'

'We do?' My father turned to look at Xavier, who sat back down on the sofa next to Catherine, both of them smiling, knees pinched together, my aunt's face tilted up towards her husband's, like she was a sunflower and he was her sun. She's thin, my aunt, not thin like maman, but thin and bony, and she wears trousers that don't stick to her arse. She was wearing a dress that day, a plain navy-blue dress that stopped at her knees and had a round collar that gave nothing away.

'So what is it, Xavier? What's your promotion?' my father asked.

'I've been made managing director,' Xavier said. He grinned and I saw what he must have looked like when he was a boy, when he was my father's big brother.

'I had no idea,' my father said as we all sat down. 'When did this happen?'

'We've been in negotiation for months, but we finally signed this week.'

'You know, Xavier, I was having lunch with Gérard this week and he said it really is remarkable for someone so young,' my grandfather said as he eased the cork from a bottle of champagne.

There was a second of silence. The air in the salon seemed to hover and vibrate. The windows were all shut tight. The clock on the mantelpiece ticked loudly. There was the release of the cork as it burst from the bottle and my father said:

'You're already boasting to your friends, Papa?'

'Not boasting, Philippe, expressing my pride. Your mother and I are very proud.' My grandfather began pouring the champagne into glasses and then Manuela passed among us with a silver tray, handing them out.

'When will it be announced?' My father's hand was shaking slightly as he put the glass to his lips.

'Next week,' Xavier said. 'At least, it should be. The contract is signed; they are deliberating on the date of the announcement. They want to get the timing right for the press in terms of the end-of-year results.'

'Of course,' my father said and he reached forward to take one of the green olives that were in a glass bowl on the coffee table.

'It's going to shake up the industry, the fact that you are so young,' my grandfather said.

'Oh, Papa,' Xavier said, 'you exaggerate. I'm not so young any more and besides, there are others my age.'

'Perhaps it's me that's growing old,' my grandfather said and he smiled at the idea.

There was a gap in the conversation. The cousins sat quietly, looking down at the carpet. They only ever spoke when spoken to. Catherine crossed her legs. She had fine hairs that lay flat beneath her beige tights, long brown hairs; they hugged her calf, and I wondered what it would be like to touch them. I wished maman were there. She would say something and detonate the tension, make it explode so we wouldn't just be sitting in this room of strangled silence.

'Nice olives,' my father said.

'Aren't they good?' my grandmother said. 'I get them from the little Arab on the boulevard, he brings them back from Algeria when he goes.'

There was another silence. My cousins sat on the edge

of their chairs, all three dressed in blue shirts and chinos, Docksiders on their feet. I sat next to my father on the sofa, facing Xavier and Catherine.

'How were your holidays, Paul?' Catherine said to me. 'I hear you were in La Baule.'

'Isn't it funny,' my grandmother interjected before I had a chance to reply, 'when you think how Séverine hated coming to Dinard when you were married and now she chooses to go to Brittany for her holidays.'

'La Baule's not really like Dinard,' I said, and my grand-parents, Catherine, and Xavier all laughed out loud.

'We can be thankful for that,' my grandfather said. He smiled to his audience. My grandmother stood up and clasped her hands in front of her breasts.

'Shall we go through for lunch?' she said.

Manuela brought in plates of smoked salmon with small mounds of white mousse on top. The mousse had a hairy green herb in it that got caught in my teeth. I tried to scrape the mousse off the salmon, but then I looked up and saw my grandmother was watching me. My grand-father was talking to Augustin, my eldest cousin, asking about the trip he was going on to see the Pope in Rome. Manuela brought in the coquilles Saint-Jacques and everyone raved and my grandmother said they came from La Rochelle. Everything has to come from somewhere with my grandmother.

My grandfather asked Augustin who would be leading the trip and then they all talked about people they knew from their school, priests and families, I don't know, just people who they knew and who meant nothing to me. I wasn't listening anyway; I was trying not to be noticed as I got another piece of bread. There was still some melted salty butter on my plate left over from the coquilles Saint-Jacques and I wanted to mop it up. It had started to harden and the yellow grease broke like a wave over my bread.

'Paul,' my father said.

I looked up. I was going to be told off for using my bread to mop up.

'Your grandfather just asked you a question.'

'He did?' I said.

'How is your maths?' My grandfather was looking at me. He must have asked my cousins the same question, because I could see by the way they were smiling that they were out of danger.

'OK,' I said.

'What is your average?'

'My average?' I said. 'My average in maths?'

'Yes,' my grandfather said.

I glanced around the table; everyone was looking at me. Even Manuela was watching me as she cleared away the plates.

'I got seventeen out of twenty in my last test,' I said.

'Seventeen?' He looked shocked, which was not surprising, given that he was used to single digits from me.

'Yeah,' I said, 'seventeen.'

I held his gaze.

'That's very good, Paul. You've made a lot of progress. That must be all the work you are doing with your new tutor. I am pleased. You have to master maths, Paul, if you want to conquer the world. And by conquer the world I mean, of course, engineering.'

Bastard I thought. He does it every time, bigs up Xavier like he's Jesus Christ just because he did engineering school. The triangle of flesh at my father's throat turned red. He jutted out his jaw. His legs were crossed and I saw his left foot bang up and down against his right leg. I wondered if he knew he was doing that.

'You didn't tell me you got seventeen.' His voice was strained.

I bit into my bread so that I wouldn't have to say anything else.

'It looks like you've got some competition, Thibaut,' my grandfather said to my cousin, who was in the same year as me at school. 'Paul is catching up on you.' They all laughed then, everyone around the table. Except for my dad; he didn't laugh. And neither did I.

After dessert Manuela cleared the plates away. I asked Thibaut what he was getting for Christmas; he said he didn't know and then he asked me what I was getting. I told him maman was giving me a new PlayStation and then I told him every single game I was getting. I did it on purpose. He listened to it all with his mouth wide open, wet with desire. My cousins aren't allowed any kind of computer game. It was pretty fun, that part of the afternoon.

Then Catherine said to him he should practise his piano, so he sat down at the piano in the salon and started playing like he was Chopin and I went looking for another Coke. Manuela had cleared the glasses away, so I went to find one. Just as I got outside the kitchen, I heard my grandmother say:

'When will it be settled?'

And my dad said:

'I don't know; it's complicated. There's a hearing scheduled for December.'

'Why is it taking so long?'

'I told you, maman, it's complicated. She's complicated.'

'Well, I told you that from the start.'

'I know you did.' There was silence and then my grandmother said:

'It's not good for Paul, the way it's dragging on. He's put on weight. I noticed it as soon as he walked in.'

'I know that,' my father said.

'Is it Cindy? Is she overfeeding him?'

'I don't know what is going on.'

'Well, you need to find out, you need to take control of the situation.'

'How can I take control, mother? I couldn't control her when we were together, how am I going to control her now we're apart?'

'You have to talk to her.'

'We don't talk.'

'Email her, then. Get your lawyer to speak to her. Did you see the way he was eating bread at the table?'

'What can I do?' my father's voice was raised.

'He needs help. He must see someone, a nutritionist, a doctor. He needs to be on a diet, he needs rules. He has no discipline, no self-control, that's his problem.'

My hands were clammy. My armpits were cold and wet. I could smell myself, my flesh all around me. I hated my expanding body. A door opened in the corridor just ahead of me. My grandfather walked out of his study and closed the door quietly behind him. I ducked down to do up my laces, which weren't laces at all, they were Velcro fasteners, but I figured my grandfather wouldn't know the difference. My stomach folded around me as I bent down, a soft underbelly; it hung down a little. I looked up from my shoes. My grandfather looked at me and blinked a couple of times, although there was no bright light.

'Paul,' he said. 'Ah, there you are. I was just reading an interesting article on Alaska, yes, the bird life there.' He stood in front of me, not moving, poised for something.

I got the feeling he was stalling for time, trying to recover. I got the feeling I had stumbled across a jigsaw piece that I hadn't known I'd been looking for. And then I remembered coming for lunch with my grandparents – I must have been about seven – and my grandmother was washing her hands, and her diamond ring caught the light and glittered in the bubbles of the soap and I asked her who gave her the ring and she said it was my grandfather and when I asked her what for, she said:

'What for? That is a very good question, Paul. I would say for putting up with all his bêtises throughout our marriage, that is what for.'

Bêtises are the kinds of naughty things that a child does. I remember thinking that it was a pretty big diamond for putting up with someone's naughtiness. But now, as my grandfather stood looking shifty outside his study, I thought maybe his bêtises were different than what I'd imagined back then.

There was silence from the kitchen, the silence of two people who've been caught by someone while they were talking about that someone, the silence of two people holding their breath behind the door. And then my grandmother said in this really fake, bouncy voice, 'At last, the coffee is ready.'

She came out into the corridor.

'Ah, Paul, there you are,' she said, as if she'd been looking for me. 'Let's go through to the salon for coffee, shall we? Now, tell me, who do you think that is playing the piano so beautifully?'

By the time we left my grandparents' place it was dark and the prostitutes' faces were pale moons in the night. There were cars streaming by, red brake lights, legs striding down to the kerb, windows opening, eyes staring into headlights.

It was hot in the car and I felt dizzy.

'Why did you lie, Paul?' my father said. He accelerated away from the traffic lights and my head jerked back against the leather headrest.

'Why did you lie?' He asked again.

'I didn't.'

'Come on, Paul, don't expect me to believe you got seventeen, you've never scored over ten.'

'I did. Ask maman.'

'We don't talk.'

'Then you'll just have to believe me.'

He stared at the road ahead and vented his anger on the gearbox. I did get seventeen. Guillaume let me copy his paper, which was hard to do because of the calculations, but he left his paper wide open and angled towards me so I could see it. He did it in return for me letting him play FIFA on my PSP.

We sat in silence. When we got as far as the Boulevard Saint-Germain I said:

'Was your dad like that when you were young?'

'Like what?'

'Xavier this, Xavier that, Xavier for President.'

'Yes,' he said and he laughed, but not as if it was funny.

'Don't you hate him for it?'

'Sometimes.'

'And Xavier, were you jealous of him?' I asked.

He shrugged. 'It was always that way.'

He was silent for a bit and then he said:

'When Xavier was eleven and I was eight his god-father took him to the Arc de Triomphe to see the tomb of the Unknown Soldier. His godfather was in the army. I stayed at home with maman; my father was away on business somewhere. I remember when they came back late that night Xavier's godfather walked in wearing his army uniform and Xavier was wearing a navy-blue over-coat and I was there waiting in my pyjamas. Xavier had been gone only a couple of hours, but it felt like some-how he'd turned into a man and there I was, still at home with maman, still a boy. He was all excited when he walked through the door. "It was me, maman," he said, "it was me that lit the flame." There's a ceremony, you see, every night at the tomb to light the flame, and somehow Xavier's godfather had fixed it so that Xavier got to light the flame.'

He drove for a bit without saying anything and then he said:

'It was always Xavier. He was the light and I came after. That's all.'

I wondered if he meant that's all as in it's no big deal or that's all as in that is the whole problem, the story of my life and the thing I will never get over. I felt sorry for him then. I wondered if the real disappointment in my dad's life was not so much me as a son but him as a son never having been the light of his father's life.

We drew up outside our apartment building and he parked, but he kept the engine running. He said nothing, just sat there, staring into the dark, looking sad. Finally he said:

'I should go.'

Just as he said that, there was the sound of a text arriving. I looked down at his phone lying in the niche between our seats. I saw the words on the screen between us.

'Come back big boy. I'm gonna treat you mean.'

I remember that is exactly what it said. I felt a strange flush stir within me. Something forbidden. My dad snatched up the phone.

'Some weirdo keeps sending me these texts and I don't know who it is. They keep arriving.'

He tried to put the phone away in his jacket, except the phone must have got caught up in the lining or something because he had to try a couple of times to jam it down inside.

'Have you told the police?' I asked.

'What's the point? They are just texts.'

'Isn't there a number?'

'Unidentified.'

'Maybe it's Irinka,' I said and I imagined an icy blonde with a gun against my father's head.

'Oh god, Irinka. I was supposed to call her.' He made a sound in his throat as if he was trying to cough out a laugh. 'You don't want to upset a Russian,' he said.

'When will I see you?'

'In a week. We'll do something fun, see a film. You should go in now, Paul.' He waited in the car while I put in the code and pushed open the wooden door to our building, then I heard him drive away.

I went upstairs to the apartment. Maman's bedroom door was open, but no one was there. The door to Lou's bedroom was closed. I could hear the sound of the steam iron and Cindy talking in Filipino. I found her in the kitchen. She kissed the screen the way she always does when she says goodbye to her kids.

'You want some hot chocolate, Paul?' She was wearing her pyjamas and her Minnie Mouse slippers; she had black mouse ears sticking out from each foot. 'I've been waiting for you,' she said.

8

Scarlett and I didn't sit together in school, but I saw her in the corridor waiting to go into lessons and in the court-yard during breaks. She didn't wait for me after school; she said she couldn't because that's when she met up with Stéphane to go to the jardin. She messaged me, though, and once when she was ahead of me in the queue at the baker's she turned to me and said: 'Do you remember the swings, Paul?'

She'd drawn around her eyes with eyeliner. Her face looked dull against the painted black lines. She had bitten down her fingernails and the skin around them was pink and a little bloodied.

The days were getting shorter and by the time I got out of school it was almost dark. Every week the Jardin du Luxembourg closed earlier and earlier and soon I could hear the guards whistling people out of there as I walked home alone. I wondered where Stéphane and Scarlett went now that they couldn't make out in the jardin.

Then one Wednesday afternoon, about four weeks after La Baule, I found Scarlett waiting for me when I came out of school. We got out early on Wednesdays. She told me she wanted to get a new cover for her phone on the Rue de Sèvres. She asked did I want to come. We didn't take the bus; we walked. I asked her where Stéphane was and she told me they had broken up. He'd started going out with Inès, Scarlett's best friend, and Scarlett had found out on Facebook. Inès has a big red mouth and a mole above her lip. The boys talked about her body and what they wanted to do to it, not as much as they talked about Scarlett's, but Inès's popularity was gaining as her breasts grew.

'It was after Dubai,' Scarlett said. 'I knew something was going on. I phoned a medium and she told me there was danger all around me. I should have listened to her. I thought he'd met some girl in Dubai, and all the time it was Inès. She borrowed my top and she wore it to go out with him. And she was always telling me he's a user. "He's using you, Scarlett, you'll see."' Scarlett sobbed a little. 'It's not possible. They're all over Facebook together and she's wearing my top from Zara.'

We walked on in silence while she texted and then after a while she said:

'How's that little sister of yours?' She sounded like an adult when she said that, like a teacher or someone old.

'She's OK,' I said.

'Have you got a photo?'

'No.'

'I want to come and see her one day.'

I looked at her to see if she was joking, if she really meant it.

'I love babies,' she said.

We had to queue for ages at the phone shop so that

Scarlett could buy a cover with Hello Kitty on it. It was three o'clock by the time we came out. We crossed into the little park right below my dad's apartment. I could see the darkened windows of his salon and bedroom. I didn't tell Scarlett my dad lived up there. We sat on the bench near the carousel. I used to spend so long on that carousel when I was small, going around and around in the orange jeep with the flashing light on its roof. Sometimes I chose the motorbike. Maria was my nanny then; she used to stand next to me, stamping her heels on the gravel, checking her watch, her phone. 'They won't be long now,' she would say. My parents were off eating lunch or brunch somewhere, or shopping on the Rue du Bac. I never really knew where they were.

'What do you want to do now?' Scarlett asked.

'I don't know.'

'I can take you somewhere, but you can't tell anyone.' She was looking at me in a strange way.

'Why not?'

'It's secret. Special.' We were right opposite Le Bon Marché and they already had their Christmas window displays up and I thought she must mean Santa's grotto or something like that.

'It's somewhere, you know, holy,' she said.

'I thought you hated Catholicism and all that stuff.'

'This isn't Catholic. Well, it is, but it's different. It's soft Catholic.'

'Like soft porn,' I said. It was a joke, but she didn't laugh.

'Do you want to come or not?'

She didn't wait for an answer; she turned away and walked on ahead and I followed her.

There was fake snow falling in the department-store windows and automated penguins and polar bears waving at us. We passed the sales assistants on their breaks, standing around in the cold wearing thin black suits, their mouths held tight, sucking on cigarettes. Scarlett turned left on the Rue du Bac; I was a few steps behind. We walked a little way and then she stopped by a bunch of gypsy women who were begging in an open doorway. One of them was wearing a long black skirt covered in green and orange parakeets. She was young, about sixteen, with a baby strapped to her chest and her hands pressed together as if she was in prayer.

She took a step towards me, but Scarlett grabbed my wrist and pulled me through the gypsies and their outstretched hands and into a long, cobblestoned courtyard open to the sky. There were people everywhere. They were staring at the courtyard walls that were covered in plaques, neat white rectangular plaques that said Thank you, Mary. Hail Mary for the gift of life. Thank you to the Virgin who answered my prayers.

I followed Scarlett and the plaques and the trail of excitement leading somewhere. Scarlett pulled open a door and I smelled incense, not fresh and burning, but stale incense that was always there. There was a knot of people stuck in the doorway, all trying to get into the chapel at the same time, black people, white people, Filipinos, old nuns in white, young nuns in navy blue, South Americans, a tour guide with an umbrella, a woman wearing a sari with jade-green rosary beads in her hand. Inside there were so many people that the chapel hummed. We sat down on a wooden pew and I listened to the hum.

It felt safe in there. It felt like Cindy's room. It wasn't like the church we used to go to with my junior school, which was huge and dark and there was a sculpture of Jesus carrying a big black cross on his back, looking up at the sky as if he was searching for God but would never find him.

Here, everything was light. There were shimmery golden mosaics and the ceiling was painted sky blue with white clouds and gold and white stars. There was a big white statue of the Virgin Mary standing on a puffy white ball of cloud that stuck right out of the wall. She was wearing a high gold crown that had two flaming gold hearts at the front and there was a halo of electric-light stars that went all the way around her head. I really loved that. She had these rays coming out of her hands. They were gold metal with bits of diamanté or something that glittered and they shot out of her hands and went straight down into the cloud ball below.

There were women everywhere: in the pews beside me, and on the walls, sculptures and paintings of women and angels, soft-mouthed women with love in their smiles, their arms held out to me. And the Virgin Marys were not the sad, black-eyed Virgins you get in other churches; they were floaty white Virgins, electric-light Virgins. Golden-hearted Virgins.

A side door opened and a priest walked in and came and stood at the front.

'The Lord is here,' he said and he raised his arms into the air. His green cassock lifted up and I could see his jeans beneath, not cool jeans, but ironed jeans, the kind you buy in Monoprix.

'Search for his pardon, beg for his pardon,' the priest said. 'Pray for his pardon, for he alone can accept our sins.'

He kept going on about preparing ourselves now for the life after, repenting now, repenting of all our sins. Then something started happening at the front; the priest was handing out the bread. At my grandparents' church in Neuilly, when they hand out the Communion, it takes for ever and everyone queues and looks depressed. Here people went rushing to the front, rushing like it was hot bread and it would run out. Nobody waited their turn; they all stood up and ran.

There was an old guy in front of us who looked like he was a waiter from the Flore – he was dressed in black and white – and he knelt in the aisle for the whole service. He had wooden rosary beads around his neck and he was so thin that when he bent forward to pray, I could see the tendons under his skin, sticking out of the back of his neck, holding his head onto his body. He went up to take the bread and so did Scarlett. I stayed in the pew. I only wanted to look at the Virgin and her soft mouth.

'A woman of most excellent obedience'; that is what the priest called her.

When the waiter guy came back from Communion, he lay down in the aisle and kissed the floor; his lips met the cold white marble and his legs stretched out behind him. I wondered why he did that. He was wearing leather sandals and no socks and it was December.

'He's a pilgrim,' Scarlett whispered, as if that explained his bare ankles and his body lying flat on the floor.

Most people left the chapel straight after the bread. But Scarlett didn't move; she sat there staring straight ahead, so I did the same. She sat there while the priest walked out and left by the same side door he had entered from. Navy-blue nuns started blowing out candles and moving furniture about. But Scarlett kept staring, like she was in a trance or something. And then finally she said:

'Do you want to see Saint Catherine?'

She led me up to a glass box at the front of the chapel.

'That's her,' she said, pointing to the box. 'That's Saint Catherine.' The woman inside was old and dead and lying flat on her back with a funny white triangular hat on her head that fanned out from her forehead. Her hands were held together in prayer. I put my face up to the glass. She was wearing black shoes. I was glad I hadn't been the one to put the shoes on her feet.

'When she died they buried her and then ages after, they dug her up again and her body was intact, it was just like the day they buried her. Her arms and legs were dangly, not rigid, and she hadn't decomposed. Then they knew she was a saint. Because she was intact.' Scarlett's eyes were funny when she said that, glittery and wide, like she really believed that stuff.

'How does that make her a saint?' I said.

'An angel appeared to her when she was a child and told her to get up and come to this chapel and when she came in, the Virgin was here and she told Catherine to sit down with her and they talked all night. Mary gave her a medal, a miraculous medal. After that, miracles started happening here. That's why people come to pray to the Virgin and to Saint Catherine. People who are ill or sad or dying, people who want babies, they are all praying for a miracle.' Scarlett wiped a tear from her eye.

'That's the chair the Virgin sat on,' she said and she pointed to a blue velvet armchair behind the altar rail. It looked just like a normal chair. 'I sat on it once when no one was looking. Everyone hopes they'll be the one to see her again, you know, like in Lourdes.' Her voice was wistful. 'I wish I could meet the Virgin.'

It must be nice to believe; it must be a comfort to think, no matter how crap your life is, somebody loves you, like Cindy believes in Jesus. She thinks he's watching over her, that he is there every day, every hour of her life.

After that we hung around in the courtyard for a bit. Scarlett went into the shop and I looked at all the plaques. I counted ninety-eight plaques saying thank you to Mary. I walked to the doorway and looked out; the gypsy women had been replaced by gypsy men.

'They do shifts,' Scarlett said, coming up behind me. 'They all want to beg outside here because there are loads of poor people who come to the chapel and poor people are the ones who give the most money. So they have to take turns. That's what it said in a documentary I watched.'

'Do you come a lot?'

'After school sometimes. At the weekends. When I'm feeling down. I just sit here on my own. I like thinking one day Mary will come.'

We walked home by the Rue d'Assas. Scarlett told me that her parents were threatening to send her to boarding school if her grades didn't improve. She told me Stéphane was posting stuff about her, talking about her body and what he had done to it, and she said that Inès was telling everyone Scarlett had given her the Zara top.

'I would never give that bitch anything,' she said. She talked about them all the way along the Rue d'Assas, non-stop, not pausing for breath.

'Do you still like him?' I asked as we stood at the lights waiting to cross the road. She stopped talking then and tears came into her eyes.

'It's not that,' she said. 'It's not being wanted, that is what hurts.'

The Rue Auguste Comte was blocked in front of the lycée. There were cones and a plastic barrier, and a police-man wearing white gloves was standing on the corner. Beyond the policeman there were navy-blue buses lined up along the road; they were packed with gendarmes. I could see their bored faces staring out at us.

'Excuse me, monsieur,' Scarlett said to the policeman. 'What is going on?'

'There's a demonstration coming from les Invalides,' the policeman said. 'We've closed the road.'

'But I live there,' Scarlett said.

'Where exactly do you live, mademoiselle?'

'Rue Saint-Jacques, the other side of the boulevard.'

'You can't pass here,' he said. 'You have to go farther down the Rue d'Assas and try cutting across there. You can't pass here.' He turned away from us.

I wanted to ask Scarlett why she'd lied to the policeman about where she lived, but she'd already broken into a run and she was jogging on ahead of me.

'Come on, Paul,' she shouted over her shoulder without slowing, 'it's going to be wild.'

I kept jogging behind her, but she ran faster than me. The streets were empty and dark. We came to Rue Michelet, but that too was blocked. She kept on running. We passed our road and I looked back along it; Cindy would be waiting.

'Wait, Scarlett!' I shouted. 'Wait for me.'

She stopped then and I caught up with her.

'Where are you going?' I said.

'There's gonna be a riot, Paul. It's the guys from the suburbs, they're going mad and smashing up Paris. I want to see them. They're burning cars and breaking shop windows. They're fighting the gendarmes and shit. They're on the rampage.'

'Why?' I said.

'Because they're sick of being kept out.'

'Kept out of what?'

'Paris. Life. It's a closed city, Paul, can't you see? It's like in the Middle Ages only now the wall around it is called the Périphérique.'

I didn't know what she was talking about.

'What do you mean?' I said.

'Don't you know anything, Paul? Don't you ever watch the news? It's the guys from the suburbs. No one's giving them jobs because they're Arabs. No one wants them. They are stuck out in the housing estates and we don't want to know. Sarkozy says they're scum. So now they hate us, they hate Paris. They want to burn Paris, they want to prove they count, prove they're alive. Don't you ever dream of smashing things up, Paul?' She had that glittery look in her eyes again.

She started running and I did too. We came to the corner of Rue des Chartreux and Rue d'Assas, where Kayser is. There were a couple of people heading home after buying their evening baguettes. They looked scared when they saw us running towards them. Scarlett turned onto Rue des Chartreux; the road was wide open, there was no police block.

She looked at me; she must have sensed my doubt.

'Listen, Paul, I'm not missing the only exciting thing that's ever happened in the 6ème arrondissement. You go home if you want. I'm going to watch.'

I was scared. I didn't want to watch what Scarlett wanted me to watch, not unless it was on my screen. But I couldn't leave her; Scarlett was a Pied Piper leading me along the road. And so I ran behind her along the Rue des Chartreux, past the niches in the red-brick wall where the homeless make their beds, past their sleeping bags and folded cardboard, past the wall smeared with shit. I would have followed her to the end of France if she'd asked me to, I would have walked to Marseille with Scarlett. She only had to ask.

The Jardin d'Observatoire was already locked, so she climbed over the first low metal gate we came to and then the next and I followed her in. No one was playing table tennis. No one was about, only a homeless guy in a black overcoat sitting on a bench. I could smell him as we walked by. He was pouring sugar into his mouth from a pink and white cardboard carton. The sugar spilled out of his mouth and onto his lips. There were crystals of it, wet and white, caught up on his black beard. He closed his eyes. I knew that pleasure.

We crossed the narrow jardin into the play area for little children. It had changed since I used to come here. They had made the floor bouncy underfoot and they'd taken away the rocking horse and put in a rocking bird instead. There were more gendarme buses parked up on the road on the other side of the hedge. The men had got out of the buses and were lined up waiting outside, stand-ing all along the road. There must have been at least fifty of them. They were wearing a kind of black armour, with breastplates and leg protection and big plastic shoulders; they had truncheons hanging from their waists. They all looked like Iron Man.

Some of them had helmets on; others wore little cloth hats, like they wear at KFC, pushed down over shaved heads. They were chatting and smoking, leaning up against the walls, waiting under the streetlights. We crouched down behind the hedgerow; it smelled of piss. We stayed like that for a while, fifteen, maybe twenty minutes, crouching in the kids' play area until my legs ached. Scarlett kept messaging people to tell them where she was.

Then one of the guys threw his hand up in the air and motioned the others forwards like they were going into battle.

'Unit 14,' he shouted. 'We're moving out.'

He had a big black moustache and he was shaped like one of those fighting dogs security men have on the RER, only he didn't have a muzzle. He was shouting orders, telling some to wait, others to move fast. It was the guys with helmets who were moving off, about thirty or so of them, jogging in formation.

'Onto the boulevard,' he ordered. 'They are coming.'

Scarlett grabbed my arm.

'Can you hear that, Paul?'

There was the sound of running boots as the gendarmes jogged together down a small side street that led from the Avenue de l'Observatoire onto the Boulevard

Saint-Michel. All the demonstrations come down the Boulevard Saint-Michel, all the strikes, the unions, gay pride, techno pride, they all take the same route. I'd seen gay pride before, loads of guys dressed in leather and feathers dancing on top of floats with booming sound systems, but this was different. There was an eerie noise coming from the boulevard, the hooting of car horns and drums beating, the sound of banging on metal, and there was a roar I had never heard before.

'Let's go,' Scarlett said. She started running towards the noise, out of the play area and along the wet sandy path. I followed her to the metal gate and then we stopped and stared at the road in front of us. There was a white vehicle parked at the end of the road where it joined the Boulevard Saint-Michel. It looked like a kind of military tank with metal wings, and the gendarmes stood on either side of it, forming a blockade behind tall plastic shields, stopping the rioters from breaking off the boulevard.

The blue buses in front of us were empty; all the gendarmes were deployed and out on the streets.

Scarlett started to climb over the metal gate.

'What the fuck are you doing?' I said. 'You can't do that.'

I was inside the gate and Scarlett was on the other side. Her back was to me.

'Look,' she said in a whisper, 'they're here.'

Just beyond the barrier of the gendarmes we could see rioters running and shouting, throwing stones, surging along on foot. The white vehicle turned on its headlights, blinding white, like prison searchlights, and the rioters put their hands up to shield their eyes. All the residents on the side street were out on their balconies looking down, watching as the neighbourhood exploded around them. I remember one of them, a guy, was standing on his balcony on the second floor, holding a glass of wine in his hand, as the gendarmes clashed with the crowd below.

And then somehow a couple of the rioters broke through the barricade at the end and suddenly they were running down the side street towards us.

'Scarlett,' I shouted, 'they're coming!' I reached across the gate and tried to pull her arm, but she shook me off and stood watching as the two guys smashed their way through the gendarmes. They were charging bulls, heads lowered and wearing motorcycle helmets with the visors pulled down, so you couldn't see their faces. One of them was carrying this big metal bar and he was striking out at the gendarmes as he ran, and there was a third guy, I hadn't noticed him before, he was running backward down the street just in front of the two charging bulls.

'Scarlett!' I shouted again and then I threw myself down into the bushes just behind the metal fence and lay in the sour leaves. Seconds later she crashed down beside me.

'He's filming it,' she said, 'that's what the guy's doing, filming on his phone.'

She was scared, I could see that, but at the same time

she wanted this, she wanted it all to blow up around her. She wanted the sky to fall in on us in the 6ème. We pressed together as we heard them near us, her chest against my chest, her hair in my mouth. They jumped over the metal gate that Scarlett had jumped over seconds before.

There was a whoop and then a voice shouted.

'Did you see that? Did you get that? I smacked his fucking head in.'

'Where are we?' another voice said and then someone called out, 'They're coming.'

They started running again, I don't know where. We heard the gendarmes running too, heavy boots down the side of the jardin, along the pavement, just on the other side of the fence. 'Going down into the RER,' a voice shouted.

We lay next to each other. Scarlett was breathing in short shallow gasps. We listened to the drumbeat on the boulevard, the screams and shouts, the crashing of metal and the hooting of horns.

After a while she said: 'They've gone.'

We stood up cautiously. She had dirt on her white jeans. My hip was grazed from where I'd thrown myself to the ground. Scarlett brushed down her jeans and I turned to look again at the boulevard. The gendarmes had managed to reseal the entrance to the side road. Beyond the riot shields, there was smoke rising on the boulevard and the rioters were still running, still fighting. But there were fewer of them. The headlights from the vehicle illuminated their bodies, lit up the smoke around them, so they appeared like figures on a stage, like gladiators fighting.

'It's too beautiful,' Scarlett said and she was right; it was beautiful. '*Putain*,' she said. 'Why can't it be like this every day?'

9

I'd never had a friend like Scarlett before, someone who really cared. I'd had guys who hung out with me, who went to the canteen with me or who sat next to me in lessons, but Scarlett was different.

By the time I woke up there were seven messages waiting from her. Every day. She sent me tons of stuff – jokes and films, photos, texts. She sent cute pictures of puppies wearing Christmas hats, videos of white fluffy kittens hanging off branches, photos of chimpanzees hugging. Constantly. She sent me videos of cars upside down and on fire, police helicopters circling the housing estates, faceless guys in hoodies hanging out in the black of night.

'Too cool,' she wrote beside the videos she sent me.

'Look at this,' with masses of exclamation marks.

I think she dreamed of finding those guys we had seen, of joining their gang, of running through the streets, throwing petrol bombs through the air. That is what she wanted.

We hung out every break time. The guys in my class asked if I was going out with her and when I said I wasn't, they called me gay. A week after we'd been to the chapel and seen the rioters on the Boulevard Saint-Michel I asked

Scarlett if she wanted to come back to my apartment and she said yes.

Gabriel was there when I opened the door; I wasn't expecting to see him. He was lying on the sofa in the salon, drinking a bottle of beer and playing on my Wii.

'Hey, Scarlett,' he said as we walked through the door, 'nice hat.'

She was wearing a knitted beanie with the word Queen embroidered in black across the front. She turned to me and said: 'Where's your bedroom, Paul?' She was chewing gum.

'Don't you guys want to watch me play Federer?' Gabriel asked.

'Nope,' she said.

She walked ahead of me into my bedroom. She lay down on my bed and did stuff on her phone. I don't know what she did. She took photos of herself, I know that, she was always taking photos of herself that she posted or sent round. I don't know who she sent them to.

She spent for ever on her phone and I sat playing on mine. Then all of a sudden she looked up and said:

'I stopped eating last summer.'

'What?' I said. I remembered the cookies and salami piled up on her breakfast plate in La Baule. 'What did you do that for?'

She shrugged. 'I wanted to see if anyone would notice.'

'How come you didn't die?'

'Well, I did eat half an apple a day, half a Granny.' That's what people call Granny Smith apples in France.

'What happened?'

'I got really thin and after a while I wasn't hungry any more. The emptiness felt good, like I was winning. But then my parents stopped me.'

She said her parents took her to a doctor and the doctor made her go to a psychiatric hospital in the 16ème. She told me she lay in a bed under a blue light for two weeks and then they told her to go home.

'You don't believe me, do you, Paul?' she said, narrowing her eyes. 'You think I'm lying.'

I didn't know what to think. She held up her phone for me to look at. She'd pulled up a hospital home page with a photo of a big glass building and a tagline above it that said: 'Welcoming adolescents from twelve to twenty with acute mental health needs.'

'You see,' Scarlett said.

Then I heard the front door open and Cindy knocked on my bedroom door.

'Are you OK, Paul?' she said; I opened the door, and she was there holding Lou in her arms.

Scarlett jumped off the bed and ran over to them.

'Lou,' she said, 'at last. Your brother's been hiding you from me.'

Cindy turned Lou around so that she was facing Scarlett, holding her up by her armpits and bobbing her up and down. Scarlett leaned in close to her face.

'You're gorgeous, Lou,' she said. At first Lou just looked at her the same way she always looked at me, blank and flat-faced. But then Scarlett made her voice go sweet and gurgly and she said Lou's name over and over until Lou's face opened up into a smile. I'd never seen Lou smile like that. It was like a flower unfurling. It started with her mouth, but then it went up into her eyes and then she started making a noise at the back of her throat, cooing at Scarlett, and she curled her tongue at the same time and she wiggled her toes.

'Can I hold her?' Scarlett said to Cindy.

Cindy passed Lou to Scarlett, carefully, like she was a vase. Scarlett held Lou close to her; she nestled her face in Lou's neck.

'You smell so good,' she said.

Gabriel was still in the salon. I could see him playing tennis on the Wii, jumping up and down and swearing at the screen. Scarlett was asking Cindy which brand of milk she gave Lou and how many bottles she drank a day.

'You're lucky, Lou, do you know that? Paul and I had carcinogenic bottles made with Bisphenol A that leaked into our bloodstream because the bottles were heated up in the microwave. We'll probably be dead by the age of thirty. But you, Lou, you'll be OK because lovely Cindy has got you the new bottles.' Scarlett spoke to Lou like she could understand.

'Is that true?' I said.

'Don't you know that? All those plastics that leach BPA and give you cancer, they're everywhere. You shouldn't keep your Evian bottle in the car because it heats up in the sun and then, man, you are cooked.'

'I never knew that,' I said.

'Hey, Scarlett,' Gabriel called from the sofa. 'Did you see that shot? I've got him on the run now. Watch out, Federer, I am onto you.'

Scarlett had her back to Gabriel and she didn't turn around. She kept talking like she hadn't heard.

'She looks like you,' she said to me.

'She does not.'

'Yes, she does. Look at her eyes. She's got your eyes.'

'How can she have my eyes?'

'She's got my eyes,' Gabriel shouted from the salon, 'everyone says she's got her daddy's eyes.'

Scarlett ignored him.

'She's going to be beautiful when she's older,' she said.

I tried to imagine what Lou would look like when she was older. I tried to imagine maman then. I thought of those other mothers who wait at the school gates on Fridays. They watch as their daughters saunter out of school, teenage hair pouring down one shoulder, teenage bodies ripe for the picking. They look sad, those mothers. They sit high up in their Range Rovers. They look like they have lost something they won't find again.

Gabriel let out a roar from the salon.

'Man, I lobbed him. Did you see that?' He took a swig of beer. 'I lobbed Federer, can you believe that? I am pumping!'

I could see the TV screen from my bedroom door and I watched as Federer walked back to the baseline with his head down. Then he turned and looked back over his shoulder, like he too couldn't believe he'd been lobbed by Gabriel. I felt sorry for Federer.

'I gotta go,' Scarlett said, checking her phone.

'You can't leave me now,' Gabriel called out, holding his arms open wide to her. 'Not now that I'm in with a chance. Don't leave me, Scarlett. I need you.'

She didn't say anything. She stayed where she was in my bedroom with Lou in her arms, but I saw her face crack open. I saw her smile.

She went away that weekend. She had to go and see her grandparents. She complained all Thursday and Friday about going, saying how boring it was there, how she would miss me. I was supposed to stay with my dad that weekend, but he had a race on somewhere, so I was at home. I got up late on Saturday. The apartment was dark and silent. Maman was out getting her hair done. Gabriel was out. Cindy was out somewhere with Lou, I don't know where. I sat in my room for a bit. I watched TV. I got up and wandered through the apartment.

Everything was perfect, the way maman likes it. The silk cushions were plumped up on the sofa; the books were lined up straight on the coffee table. I've never seen her read those books, but the first thing she does when she gets home from work at night is go into the salon and move them a centimetre to the right or the left, as if she can't rest until that's done. Then sometimes she calls the florist to ask why he hasn't been by to change the roses. Or she'll run her finger along the lacquer surface of the coffee table and call to Cindy to come in and remove a fingermark that she can see; she kind of worships that coffee table.

Cindy is always polishing, tidying, cleaning. It's a full-time job keeping the apartment perfect. I'm not allowed to touch the walls, because that way they stay white. Maman has them painted once a year. Cindy is constantly tidying stuff away. The out-of-season clothes get packed in boxes. Maman has a whole room for storing the clothes that she is not wearing. It's the *chambre de bonne* next to Cindy's, up on the sixth floor; it's the same size as Cindy's room. Maman wants everything pristine, everything in order; it makes me think of a rubber band stretched tight.

I got a message then from Scarlett telling me she was on the A11, heading west. I thought maybe I could go to the Chapelle de la Médaille Miraculeuse again, that it would make the day go quicker. I walked all the way along the Rue d'Assas. I saw the doors to Scarlett's apartment building were open, so I looked in, just in case, but there was no one there, just an empty courtyard. I got as far as the corner of Rue du Bac and Rue de Babylone. I stood for a bit watching people going in and out of Le Bon Marché. I let the department-store air blow over me as the doors swung open and shut. It was warm and perfumed. The yellow shop lights stained people's faces as they stepped back out into the daylight. They were Christmas shopping, coming out loaded up with orange carrier bags.

I could smell roasted chestnuts; there was a guy selling them from a barrel at the entrance to the park below my dad's place. I bought myself a packet of caramel-coated peanuts and I went and sat in the park on my own. I didn't want to go to the chapel without Scarlett. She kept messaging me, sending me a running commentary of her journey – what she'd had for lunch, the row with her mother. Paris was empty without Scarlett.

I sat on the bench and watched the carousel and I sucked the caramel off my peanuts. I watched the parents lifting their kids onto the motorbikes and jeeps. I looked up at my dad's apartment. There was a light on in the salon and another light in his bedroom. It was probably Essie cleaning. She must get so bored; there was hardly anything to clean in there.

Essie had lent me some keys a couple of weeks before; she'd said, you never know when you might need them. I don't know why she said that. I never went round to my dad's if he or Essie weren't there. It was strange, thinking I was a guest in my dad's apartment. They don't tell you that when they break up, they don't say from now on you can come and see me only when I decide you can, or when your mother lets you, but basically that is the reality.

The keys were in my pocket. I didn't usually carry them because I was worried I'd lose them, but I had them with me that afternoon. I put my hand in my jeans pocket and I turned the keys over: a flat silver key for the inner glass door downstairs and a star-shaped gold key for his apartment door. I swapped benches and went and sat further along, which meant I could see the door to his apartment building. A man went in. A white guy with a big shaved head opened the door and stepped through.

Why couldn't I go up to his apartment? Why couldn't I just go up and be there, hang out in his salon, not do anything, just sit and watch TV? Wait for him. It was getting cold; I had only my thin parka on. I could tell my dad that I'd wanted to go up and get out of the cold. He wouldn't mind.

I got up and walked out of the park. I was only going to his apartment. I waited for a break in the traffic and I ran across the road. I walked along a bit until I got to his building. I pressed the digits of the door code. I put my hand on the door to push, but it swung out in front of me. A Filipino nanny was coming out with a little boy in a grey balaclava. I helped her carry the pushchair over the step and then I went in. The concierge's lodge was dark behind lace curtains.

I unlocked the glass door with the smooth silver key. There was a Christmas tree in the hall that was lit up with white lights and gold tinsel. There were presents loaded up under the tree. They weren't real presents; they were just empty boxes, wrapped up to look nice. Teresa does that too in our apartment building. She used to put up strings of flashing coloured lights, but people in our building complained it wasn't chic.

I put my foot on the first stair. I could hear my own breathing, coming out fast and uneven. There was no noise on the staircase, not until I got to the second floor and then I heard a child crying. Third floor there was silence; fourth floor, silence. Fifth floor was my dad's floor. I thought I heard voices. I stopped to listen. Nothing.

I stood outside his door looking at the dark green paint. It was so green, it was almost black. I looked up at the metal spy hole and I imagined my dad standing on the other side of the door and looking out at me through the spy hole, seeing my face distorted with my eyes large and my cheeks gross and outsize. I heard voices again. From inside.

I put my key in the lock, the star-shaped gold key; my hand was shaking. I pressed the key in slightly and turned it just one notch to the left. The lock released, which meant someone must be home because the door had only been pushed shut. I nudged gently at the front door and it opened. I was careful not to make any sound. I heard noises from inside, not laughter, not talking.

The door to my father's bedroom was wide open. It was empty in there. The bed was made, the pillows plump, and the duvet cover smooth, not a crease. The salon doors were open. Something had happened in there, some violence had taken place, I did not know what. The magazines and books that usually lay on the coffee table had been thrown all over the floor; *Men's Fitness* was lying with its pages of big bodies splayed. There was a black vase broken on the cream rug. The water had stained the rug a dull grey and there were shards of jagged black glass sticking up and white flowers lying smashed on the floor.

I walked dazed along the corridor towards the voices.

The door to the laundry room was open just a bit. A windowless room. I stood to the side of the door, not showing myself. I stood so that I could see through the narrow gap. I saw a man. Blindfolded, I thought. No, not blindfolded, a black hood over his face. Slits for eyes. Like wrestlers wear. Behind my father. My father's chest was naked. He was wearing cycling shorts, but they were pulled down. The hooded man was punishing my father, punishing him with his sex – *son sexe*, that is what they say in French. There was sweat on my father's body, not sweat from running, sweat from fucking, from being fucked. They were animals. Hammering at each other, grappling, shouting, saying things. There were red welts on his shoulders. Beating and thrashing, that's what the man was saying. He needed taming. He needed to be taught a lesson. I could see them through the crack in the door, the laundry room with the washer and the dryer, their feet squeaking on the white tiles, my father's work shirts, washed and ironed, hanging from the rack above their heads.

I looked away. There was a blue asthma inhaler on the floor by my feet and I wondered if it was his, the man in the mask, if he had dropped it when he was putting on his mask. A leather jacket was lying there too, abandoned. I wondered what would happen if he had an asthma attack now. If he would start to cough and choke and wheeze inside the black rubber. I'll make you beg for it. I'm going to thrash you so you can't sit down. Yes, he said. Yes. I tasted my own sweat. I tasted my own tears.

I reached down and picked up the inhaler. I took some

steps backward. I put it in my pocket. I stepped on the jacket that was lying on the floor. Is this what I had been searching for?

I fell slightly against the doorjamb, knocking my shoulder. I got through the door but it made a noise as I shut it and afterward I wondered if my father had heard. I ran down the stairs, two at a time I ran down them, down the burgundy-and-gold-flowered carpet, down the stairs, the oblong descent of dark wood and polish, the black-red of the stained-glass windows. The brass banisters were green, glowing green in the overhead electric light; someone was going up in the lift. I hated that lift. It was a black lift with a wrought-iron door that closed in a concertina that would rip your arm off if it could. That is what a door like that would do in a lift like that. I burst out of the door. I was crying. I ran. Fast. I ran fast, but I couldn't keep up the pace for long. I was so unfit. I couldn't even run to the end of the road. I looked over my shoulder. He wasn't following me. He wasn't even running after me. I stopped and bent over, holding my knees, to catch my breath.

Everyone was staring at me. I was crying so much. I was sobbing. Is that what you are? Is that what you want? Is that why you left maman, why you left me, because we can't give you that? I was on the Boulevard Raspail and people were pushing past me. Those texts he got, the text on his phone that he said some weirdo was sending. I'm gonna treat you mean. All the training and his body obsession, his abs, his chest, all the pushing harder, faster, taking Didier, riding around Longchamp on his bike with his arse in the air. Begging for it. Todd. I thought of Todd, the animal man and the bulge in his shorts when he was standing in the corridor with my dad looking at my dad's phone. Maybe it was Todd under the mask – only Todd was Australian and the guy was shouting in French. Swearing in French. He told me to do better in maths, to be better, to work harder.

I walked along the Boulevard Raspail. I can't remember what I saw, I thought only about what I had seen. I'd tell my grandparents. I'd tell them over lunch in Neuilly, when Manuela was serving the cheese, when my grandmother had a salad leaf poised on her silver fork, when my grandfather was boring us all with the year and the château and the grape, when Xavier and Catherine were just back from their pilgrimage. I would tap the side of my glass and clear my throat, the way my grandfather does. You have always blamed maman, I would say, complained that she is not one of you, rolled your eyes at her clothes when we went for lunch to your tennis club in the Bois de Boulogne, called her hard-faced, demanding, said it was her fault they broke up. Well, I'm here to tell you how your son spends his weekends. Last Saturday afternoon he was not at the race he'd told me he was at; last Saturday afternoon he was getting fucked by a man. Which man? you ask. Good question. I am unable to tell you which man because he was wearing a black hood with slits for the eyes and your son, your lying son, was begging for it.

The cars were driving fast along the *quai*. I ran out between a grey car and a bus. I didn't see the taxi and he had to swerve. 'Go fuck yourself!' I shouted at him as he hooted at me. I climbed over the metal barrier on the other side of the road. The fat of my thighs squashed against the metal as I hoisted my leg up. I ripped my jeans on a spike getting over the metal. I cried out. I ran up some steps onto the bridge. I don't know which bridge; don't ask me which goddamn bridge. I stood there panting in the dark watching the Seine beneath me. Flowing fast under my feet. There were peaks of white surging on top of waves; there were smooth glassy plates of water. I had blood on my leg. It started to rain again, flooding the cone of light beaming down from the lamppost. All the shit he gave me for lying about my results. About how I had to try harder. Harder. Harder. I had tried so hard. You lied to me.

I needed Scarlett, she would help me, she would know what this was about, what it meant, she would tell me about an article she'd read or a television programme she had seen and then she would say, 'It wasn't you, Paul, it wasn't you that made this happen.'

I stood on the bridge for a long time. I stood letting the water rush beneath my feet, letting the cold air dig into me and all the yellow lights of Paris blur in my eyes. I stood until I looked down and a jacket came floating by, underneath the bridge to the right of where I was standing, near the bank; it was transported along on the flood of the river. It was a man's jacket, red-and-black checks, floating and bloated, being washed away downstream. It had the shape of arms in the sleeves, the shape of a chest in the front. It was puffed up like there was a body inside.

And I wished it were my father inside that shirt. I wished it were him, dead and floating before me, bloated, grey from being poached in the dirty rushing river, eyes wide open, looking up at me, knowing what I knew, seeing what I had seen. Thrashed to death.

10

It was too wet to stay out. My parka was soaked through and streams of water ran down inside my sweatshirt. Maman had bought me the coat in Milan when she went there for work. I thought it was pretty cool until it went all over Facebook that fur collars on parkas were made from dead dogs in China. Scarlett sent me videos of skinned dogs heaped up in piles, still writhing in pain, flapping their heads at the camera.

I looked down at the collar; the skin was exposed beneath where the wet fur had clogged and clumped in the rain. I smelled like a dead dog.

I wandered along by the Seine, looking down at the sheer drop into the river. The water lapped up against the wall on the other side of the bank and the tourist boats seemed to spin on the surface of the flood. The Tuileries was empty, washed away, bleached of colour, just bald blackened trees and white statues and grey ponds of water. The wind whipped at my body. I was so cold. Maman kept texting me, asking where I was. I knew that was the Seine beneath me, the sky above, but when I looked around for help, the grand apartments on the Quai Voltaire stared back at me, indifferent.

I crossed over the road and looked into the windows

of the *antiquaires*, lavish shops selling chandeliers and dark tapestries with unicorns and weeping ladies. There was a long black-and-white marble table that stood on heavy gold legs in the shape of bare-breasted women. On top of it there was a silver bowl of red flowers, petals the colour of blood. Everything was extravagant and elegant and I cried then because I knew it would always be this way. Paris will never change, not for you, not for me. Paris doesn't care that you are dying inside; it will always be beautiful, untouchable, aloof, unmoved by you and your pathetic fate.

The rain lashed against me and the Christmas shoppers pushed by, clutching their bags to their chests, turning their eyes away from my tears, shoving me with their open umbrellas. I turned down the Rue Bonaparte and I called Scarlett, but she didn't pick up. She messaged straightaway. She said she couldn't talk right then; she would call me back.

I had a big dead lump inside my chest that was weighing me down. It got in the way of my breathing. It expanded within me; it pressed against my lungs. It struck against my vertebrae. I don't know how I got home, because there was this dead lump making me sink, making me fall. When I got onto the Rue d'Assas, Scarlett called.

'Are you OK?' she said.

I wanted to cry out when I heard her voice. I wanted to say no, no, I am not OK. I tried to pretend I was, even when I knew I was not, but now there is a dead weight inside my chest and a dead dog around my neck and they are bringing me down. Save me, Scarlett, I wanted to say.

But instead I said, 'Yeah, I'm OK.'

'You're too lucky to be in Paris instead of stuck out in this dead man's hole. I've just had to listen to my grandparents talking about their next-door neighbour's bowel cancer.'

I kept walking. I was still breathing. I knew that because I could hear the sound of my breath echoing back at me from my phone.

'Are you there?' she asked.

'Yeah, I'm here.'

I needed to tell her. I needed someone to know. But how could I trust her?

'It's Max,' I said.

'Who's Max?'

'Estelle's son. Estelle, my mum's best friend.'

'The one with the plastic tits?'

'Yeah, her.'

'What about her?'

'Not her, it's him. Max. He walked in on his father. He walked in on his father and a man having sex,' I said.

'Oh my god!' She shouted it out, the way she shouts with her friends in the jardin when they are slamming gossip about. 'How bad is that?' She laughed out loud.

I didn't reply.

'Are you still there, Paul?' she said.

I could hear excitement in her voice; she was enjoying

the revelation, replaying it in her imagination, waiting for details.

'Yeah, I'm still here.'

'Where were they?'

'At his dad's apartment. He went round and found them in the laundry room.'

'In the laundry room? Why would you do it in the laundry room with all your dirty washing?'

'He was wearing a hood.'

'Who was wearing a hood?'

'The guy. The guy was. The guy doing it, he was wearing a black hood.'

She swore then, a whole trail of expletives that went on and on. I kept walking, staring straight ahead. She said:

'Didn't they see Max standing there? Didn't they, like, stop and say, "Oh my god, what are you doing here?"'

'No,' I said. 'They did not.' I curled my fingers around the blue inhaler inside my jeans.

'Is he gay?' she said.

'Is who gay?'

'Max's dad, who do you think?'

'I don't know. I've only ever seen him with women. He has loads of women. He's always got some new girl. He says it's easy for him to attract women.'

'Yeah,' she said to someone. 'I'm coming.' Then to me she said: 'They drive me mad. They won't leave me alone.' She broke off again and this time she shouted. 'I told you. I'm on the phone.' She sighed with frustration. 'I hate my mum. All she does is nag. I have to go. I'll message you later.'

'Yeah,' I said. 'Do that.' And then I said: 'Wait. Scarlett?'

I wanted to tell her not to tell anyone about Max.

But she'd already gone.

My grandmother's handbag was stiff and black with the letters D, I, O and R hanging off it in gold. It was sitting on top of the table in the hallway when I walked in. I heard her voice somewhere in the apartment. The water in the flower vase was cloudy. The white petals had turned oily and transparent and there was red pollen smudged across the table. Maman wouldn't be happy about that.

I found them in the kitchen, maman and her mother, one on either side of the marble island.

'Where have you been?' maman said when she saw me. 'Oh my god, what happened to your leg? Your jeans are ripped. You're soaking, take that coat off, you look terrible. Didn't you get my texts?'

She felt my forehead like I was a child.

'I went for a walk,' I said.

'He'll get ill like that,' my grandmother said.

Maman helped me take my coat off and my sweatshirt, then she threw the clothes on the counter behind her.

'Where's Cindy?' I said.

'She's gone to the supermarket,' maman said.

'He needs a bath,' my grandmother said, 'put him in a hot bath.'

'Come, Paul.' Maman led me into my bathroom and turned on the taps.

I was so cold.

'Where were you?'

'I got lost.'

'How did you get lost?' She was testing the water, trailing her hand in the bath. 'Where did you go?'

'I wanted to see the Seine.'

'The Seine? What did you want to see the Seine for? It's pouring down out there. What's wrong with you, Paul?' She touched my forearm.

'Nothing.' I shrugged. 'I'm hungry, that's all.'

She left me then and I locked the door and took off the rest of my wet clothes and I stood there naked and shivering. There was dried blood on my leg. I looked at my body in the mirror. I was fatter than before. The hairs on my legs were black and insistent. I had hairs in my armpits too, growing thicker and blacker, sprouting out of me. A bitter smell of my own sweat followed me around all the time now, like it was my new shadow. I waited until the bath was deep enough to drown in and then I lay in it and cried.

All this pain was my pain. There was no one to share it with. Even if I told Scarlett the truth, that it was me, not Max, my dad in the laundry room, not his, it wouldn't be her pain, it would just be a story she could tell, a kind of horror story that made her gasp and be thankful that it wasn't her dad.

When I went back into the kitchen, they were still standing there. Maman looked tired; her skin was purple beneath her eyes. She'd worked late the week before.

'Better now, Paul?' my grandmother said; she didn't wait for a reply. 'I've just been telling your mother about my terrible day. My car got towed away on the Rue du Bac, can you believe it? I only nipped in to pick up my coffee – of course the queues were terrible before Christmas – and then when I came out I couldn't find the car.'

Why was she even here? I wanted Cindy, not her.

'I walked up and down the Rue du Bac looking for it, I thought I was going mad, and then this man came out of the hairdresser's and he said to me, "Are you looking for a silver Golf with a Yorkshire terrier in the back?" and I said yes.'

She wouldn't stop talking.

'He said they'd taken it ten minutes ago; they took it with the dog inside. I screamed when he told me that. He said they jacked up the car and rolled it onto some kind of trailer. He said they were racing to do it, like they were in the pit at Le Mans. He saw it all with his own eyes, Chipie sitting on the ledge and looking out the back window as they towed her away. Can you believe it? It's criminal. She could have died from the shock or dehydration. I could sue them. I didn't bring her with me now. I left her at home. She's still recovering. Christophe's looking after her.'

I Love You Too Much

I wouldn't want Christophe looking after me. He is my mother's brother. She hardly ever sees him. She won't let him come to the apartment. I looked at my grandmother standing there with her black suede ankle boots and the silver zips running up the back of them and their high wedge heels that make her tip forward at an angle. She was wearing her grey fur gilet, the one she thinks makes her look young. The flesh along her jawline had come loose and her chin bulged a little underneath. She tries so hard to run after my mother, to keep her in her sights. I wished she would leave us alone. I went over to the cupboard.

'What are you doing?' maman asked.

'Just getting a DooWap.'

'Not now, Paul,' she said. 'Cindy will be back any minute, she's bringing soup.'

I didn't want soup. I wanted Cindy's rice. I wanted a massive plate of Cindy's white rice with a slab of butter in the middle and ketchup too, a dirty squirt of it, and I wanted to mix it all up, around and around, the butter chasing the ketchup until the rice turned pink and the butter left skids of golden grease on the rim of the plate and I could eat the lot and I could forget.

'I'm starving,' I said.

'The last thing you need is a DooWap,' my grandmother said.

Lou started crying from her bedroom, that special cry she uses when she wants feeding, a kind of desperate cry that makes people stop in the street and lean over the pram and look inside and wince with pity.

'She's hungry,' my grandmother said.

Maman said nothing. She hates it when you tell her Lou is hungry. She pulled open the fridge door and scanned the shelves to make out she was looking for something, when really she was just trying to hide her anger. The baby monitor was on the island and the radio version of Lou's screams joined the real live sound coming from along the corridor. She was televised too, twisting her body, bringing her legs up to her chest, scratching at her face with her fingers, milking the full drama from it.

'She's not getting enough food, Séverine,' my grandmother said. 'She's hungry. That is the real problem, not this colic you keep going on about. You did the same with Paul when he was a baby. He was always hungry. Always crying. Don't you remember?'

Maman slammed the fridge door. It should have been more dramatic but the fridge suction pads took the bang out of the slam. She turned to face her mother. There was silence between them. The only sound was Lou's screaming. And then maman said:

'And you, mother, what makes you think your child-rearing was so perfect?'

I remember the way she said the word mother, like she was throwing a punch to break my grandmother's jaw. They stared at each other across the kitchen island. The skin above my grandmother's lip was ironed flat. No matter how hard she tried, she was losing ground. Maybe getting at my mother was the only way she had of staying in the race.

'What do you mean by that?' My grandmother's smile was jaunty as she said that, trying to downplay the aggression that she had unleashed, trying to put back the pin she had pulled from the grenade.

'Oh, I don't know, mother, how about we start with the fact your son still lives in a *chambre de bonne* above your apartment and he's aged thirty-seven, how about we start right there?'

'What has Christophe got to do with this?'

'You criticized the way I bring up my children. I'm criticizing the way you brought up yours. Your son can't even cook his own supper. He's dependent, emasculated.'

'He has a job.'

'You do his washing.'

'He doesn't have a washing machine.'

'Why not, mother? Why do you think he doesn't have a washing machine?'

'It's different with a boy, they still need their mothers. You'll see one day.' She jerked her eyebrows in my direction.

My mother laughed, a harsh, bitter laugh.

'You call him a boy even though he's aged thirty-seven and divorced. I was out earning money, living on my own in Paris at nineteen, and there he is, still tucked up living above his maman.'

'You wanted to leave, Séverine, that was your choice,' my grandmother said.

'You're right.' My mother drew her lips back from her bright white teeth. 'I wanted to leave.' To get away from you. She didn't say that last bit out loud, but that is what she meant, that is what she was thinking; it was obvious from the way she was staring at my grandmother, staring so hard that it seemed any second now, two burning red laser beams would spring from maman's eyes and drill straight into my grandmother's skull.

Then out of nowhere my mother said:

'You always made me feel like I wasn't good enough for Philippe.'

My grandmother made a snorting sound. 'Nonsense, Séverine, that was you who thought that.'

'Perhaps, yes, perhaps you are right, but if I thought that, it was because you made me think that. That I was lucky to marry him.'

'Well, you were.'

'Meaning what?' my mother said.

It would be better if my grandmother shut up now. She was taking my mother to a place where they would both erupt in flames and I wasn't sure what I could do when they got there.

But she didn't shut up; she continued, her slack jaw set, her voice hard.

'Meaning you were lucky to marry him, Séverine. He was a good catch. And you caught him. Were you vigilant enough?' She raised an eyebrow as she said that.

'Why did I need to be vigilant, mother?' Maman's voice sounded like a threat.

Stop, I wanted to say to her, stop, you don't understand. You don't know what he wants. No one could be vigilant enough for him, not you, not me, not your mother. But I said nothing. I was mute and inert. I watched as my grandmother pursed her lips, opened her manicured hands, and said:

'There must be a lot of temptations along the way for a man like Philippe – handsome, rich, clever, from a good family.'

'You sound like you want to fuck him yourself, mother.'

'Don't be vulgar, Séverine.'

Maman laughed out loud, but not as if it was funny. And then she shook her head and said:

'You used to love me for being beautiful. You used to buy me dresses and do my hair and tell me all the girls at school wanted to be like me. And then you got angry; angry when I got dressed up, angry when I went out. That time we went to Naples, to that hotel where you broke your toe on the side of the bath. I was fifteen and I was wearing my new red dress that I had bought from Kookaï with my own money and when I came down, you told me I looked like a slut. Remember? We went out for pizza and there was a good-looking waiter who took our order and he was wearing a red shirt, not the red of my dress, but a deep black-red, and he leaned over me and called me Signorina when he took the menu away. I looked up and he was staring at me and you were staring at me too, maman, staring at me and hating me, I saw it in your eyes. Is that why you keep Christophe? So there is someone you can control?'

Lou had stopped crying. I held my breath and watched

my grandmother. It was like a wildlife documentary on TV, like watching the antelope being stalked by the lioness down to the edge of the water hole, and the antelope looks around with bulging eyes, waiting for the leap that she knows is coming, for the tearing of claws into her own flesh. But then my grandmother laughed out loud, not a real laugh, a brittle Disney laugh, and I realized that she too was a lioness.

'Enjoy it while you can, Séverine,' my grandmother said. 'You keep your grip with your personal trainer, your dermatologist, your teeth bleaching, your work-outs, your detox diets. You've got Lou in her baby clothes and cashmere, oh, how you love it, the Bonpoint outfits, the Liberty blouses – don't think I haven't seen you styling her like she's a model at one of your fashion shoots. But wait until the day when she wears her red dress and her breasts are full, not fake, not inserted by some surgeon, wait until she is young and desirable. Wanted.' She spoke slowly, relishing every word. 'Then it will be you watching the waiter and he will see only her.' She paused to take a breath. 'No one will look at you then, Séverine. Or if they do, it is only as the well-preserved mother of Lou. It will be Lou who is the object of desire, Lou who is the one everyone wants, her beauty, not yours, on the métro, on the terrace of the cafe, every day, everyone staring at her, not you, and no amount of clothing or money or dieting will change that. Wait until you feel that pain. Wait until all your power has gone.'

My mother stared at her mother. I stared too, transfixed by her strange, triumphant smile.

'*Voilà*, Séverine, when you know that moment, then perhaps you too will have need of your son.'

There was silence.

A key turned in the service door just behind us. It was Cindy, loaded up with shopping bags from Ed l'épicier. The smell of rubbish bins followed her up the tradesman's staircase.

'Good evening, madam,' she said to my grandmother. 'Hello, madam. Hello, Paul.' She was smiling. 'There was no washing-up liquid, madam, I looked everywhere, but there was none. I got some product for sir's ironing.'

Maman said nothing.

'I must go,' my grandmother said, her voice sharp and pointy. She didn't kiss us goodbye. She leaned forward slightly on her wedges and walked slowly and deliberately down the corridor, taking care not to pitch over onto her face. We heard the slam of the front door, and then Lou started crying again.

'I go, madam,' Cindy said. 'I give her the bottle.'

Maman didn't protest. Her thumbs were all over her phone screen.

'Where are you? You are never there when I call,' she said into her phone, and then in another voice, a pleading voice, she said: 'Call me back, won't you?'

She went over to the window. The apartment opposite was in darkness. She stood by the window and wept.

I wanted to go to her, but I didn't know how to reach her. I didn't know what I could say that would comfort her. So I stood and watched with the dead lump in my chest and my hands hanging down by my sides.

11

I looked it all up. I looked up the sites. I saw the images. I watched the videos of men doing it. I let their bodies and faces flash before me, I let their cocks beat at the screen until I couldn't watch anymore. I spent hours on my laptop. I watched it all.

Later that night, my father texted me.

'How've you been?' he wrote.

I read it so that he would know I'd read it.

I wanted him to feel uneasy. I wanted him to remember the sound of a door shutting somewhere in the apartment.

Half an hour later, he texted me again.

'Are you OK, Paul?'

After it was over and the man had taken off his hood, did he turn to my father and say:

'*Merde*, I've lost my inhaler, it must be here somewhere. I really need it for my asthma. I get chronic asthma, you see.'

Did they get down on their hands and knees then? Did they scrabble across the parquet side by side, my father with his cycling shorts pulled up, the man with his stomach hanging over the belt of his jeans, no longer animal and hard, two strangers searching through a pile of cold, discarded clothes? And later, when Essie came round, did my father say to her, 'Did you come by this afternoon, Essie?'

'Come by, sir?'

'Here to the apartment? This afternoon, I thought I heard someone.'

'Sir was waiting for me?'

'No, Essie, no, I wasn't waiting. I just wanted to know if you came by this afternoon.'

'Oh, no, sir.'

I was hungry again. I went out into the corridor. Cindy was in the kitchen polishing the surfaces.

'Where's maman, Cindy?'

'She's sleeping now,' she said. 'You want some rice?'

She took the bowl out of the fridge and put it in the microwave then she whacked on the heat until the cling-film blew into a bubble then sucked back down and the grains of rice curled up like they were in pain. She plopped it out onto a plate. It made a sticky white mound. It smelled good. She placed the ketchup and butter next to me.

'Do you like your dad, Cindy?' I said.

'I like him,' she said. She went back to rubbing the metal behind the cooker, using tiny circular movements to take the marks away.

'Have you ever hated him?'

She looked confused by that, so I tried to explain.

'I mean, hated him for something he did.'

She looked embarrassed. She laughed a little and said

nothing. I thought she hadn't understood my question. I ate the rice. She carried on polishing and then after a while she said, 'When I left the Philippines he said it was not right, what I did. He said I must stay with my children, but I said I must go to make it better. My mother said it was right. But my father did not understand. He said I was not a good mother to do what I did. He did not give me his blessing. I saved the money to come here. My family lent me money, my cousins and aunties. You need a lot of money for the ticket and the visa, you pay people and they make a visa, not a real visa, a fake visa, and then they get you in. It cost two thousand American dollars. My father didn't talk to me for a long time. After I was angry with him. Mostly I was sad. But now I send back money and he can go to hospital. He is not a fisherman any more, he has a problem with his heart.'

She stopped and looked embarrassed. I had finished my rice. I felt tired.

'Thanks, Cindy,' I said. I got up to go back to my room. It felt a little better somehow, knowing that Cindy got angry. I walked down the corridor and maman called to me from her bedroom. It was dark in there, but she was awake, sitting up and watching television.

'Where's Gabriel?' I asked.

'He's got a gig.'

'Where?'

'Lyon, you know, the big time.' She laughed. 'I wish he could just get a proper job and earn money and work regular hours and be here when I need him.'

'You should come home during the day,' I said. 'He's here all the time then.'

'What does he do all day?'

'Lies around on the sofa with his shoes on. Plays on my Wii. Phones people. He's always on the phone.'

'Nice work if you can get it.' She looked sad. She patted the bed beside her. I went and sat down.

'What are you watching?'

'Some American trash.'

We watched it for a bit together and then she said,

'What happened today, Paul?'

I kept watching the screen.

'Nothing.'

'Why did you stay out like that, getting soaked?'

'I just felt like it.'

'Is everything OK at school?'

'Yeah.'

'You're not being bullied?'

'No.'

'You're not in trouble?'

'No.'

'Is it that girl from La Baule?'

I turned and faced her then.

'Why do you say that?'

'I don't know; she scares me. She's like a magpie, the way she jitters around. I saw her talking to you in the queue in the restaurant that time. There's something strange about her.'

'It's not Scarlett.'

'What is it, then?'

I was too frightened to tell her, scared that I would make her angry or that I would hurt her, make her cry again like her mother had. I thought, if I tell her, if I hand her the pain it will only take her away from me; she will curl herself up in a ball around the anguish so that it is at the very core of her and then she will roll away from me, far away, so that I can never touch her.

'I'm OK,' I said. 'I promise.'

'You would tell me?' She was looking at me, searching for clues but at the same time, I saw, she didn't want to know. She was scared I would tell her, scared that she would find out the reason.

'Yeah,' I said, 'I would.'

We sat back and watched TV and it was like the good old days, when she was on her pills and I was in her bed. Except it wasn't. Later, about an hour later, she said:

'Do you remember how it used to be? When your dad left and you stayed with me in my bed?'

'Yeah. I remember.'

'You saved me, Paul, did you know that?'

She put her arm around me; I looked up into her eyes. She was beautiful again.

'You can stay tonight,' she said, 'if you want.' She looked scared, frightened that I might not stay, that she would be alone.

She got up and went to the bathroom. I got under the duvet. I threw the top pillow onto the floor so that

I didn't have to sleep where Gabriel's face had been. I kept my clothes on. I lay down facing my mother's side. She came back wearing her satin slip and got into bed and switched off her bedside light. The streetlight outside cast a strange glow in the room; it lit up the bedroom as if it were the moon. She stroked my forehead. And I thought of my father and the hooded man. She stroked my forehead until I closed my eyes.

When I woke up, maman was gone. It was late, around midday. My leg hurt where I had torn it on the spike and I had a headache. Cindy must have gone to church. I had eighteen messages from Scarlett. She'd sent a video of a piglet in a paddling pool and a message that said: 'Save me.'

I went into the kitchen. I found a pack of four Flanbys at the back of the fridge. Cindy must have bought them for me the night before. She knows I love them. I turned the plastic container upside down on a plate and peeled away the little metal flap from the bottom of the pot so that the caramel custard flopped out. I took my spoon and mashed the custard into the syrup and kept stirring until it made a dark golden liquid that smelled synthetic and sweet.

Scarlett had sent me a Flanby video the week before. There's a whole series of them on YouTube, all the same joke showing strange dads stealing their kids' Flanbys from under their noses. I tried sucking my third Flanby off the plate the way the dad in the video did. You have to get your mouth really close to the plate and open it really wide and then gobble and suck at the same time. I opened the last remaining pot. I chased it around the plate until it was all gone. I licked the plate.

I went back into my bedroom. The mother of the girl with black hair was standing at the window opposite. She was talking on the phone, staring right into our apartment, squinting both eyes like she was trying to get a better look. Her hair was dark and wavy, pulled back in a ponytail, and her face was always red, like she'd just been slapped. She must have felt me watching her, because her gaze fell on me. She looked at me for several seconds and then she turned her back on me, like it was me that was spying.

The girl with black hair has her bedroom opposite mine; she sits at her desk hunched over a book until late at night or she lies on her bed and reads. She pretends she can't see me. Often she plays the piano in their salon. I hear her practising every Wednesday afternoon and her music echoes in the courtyard. It haunts me. I don't know why it makes me feel so lost.

I was behind her once on the street years ago when she was little and walking home with her mother. She must have asked for something more to eat because her mother turned on her and snapped: 'That's enough, I said. Do you want to be fat like an American?'

The mother finished her telephone call. I watched her switching off the lights in the salon, picking something up off a chair, adjusting the folds of the dark red velvet curtains. They don't usually stay in Paris at the weekends. They must have a place in the country. Normally as soon as the girls get back from Saturday school, their mother reverses their big blue Peugeot people carrier out of the garage; she parks it in the courtyard, and calls out to the girls to hurry. They come down with their school bags and when they are all sitting in the car and the mother has packed the boot, the father walks out of the doorway marked B carrying an old leather briefcase, wearing glasses, looking somehow more precious than the rest of them; he always sits in the front passenger seat and it is the mother who drives.

I opened my window a little. I climbed up onto my radiator so that I could look down. The courtyard was green: dark ivy weeping in the corners of the building, green moss between the cobbles, green mould at the base of the wall, even the cream of the walls looked green in the December light. It was like living underwater.

Teresa was hosing down the courtyard, spraying the cobbles and sweeping the dirty water into the drain with a broom. Her hair was grey really, but she dyed it. I could see the grey pushing out from the centre parting of her hair. It grows like that, the grey seeping further and further out, until one day I'll see her hoovering the staircase and she will lift her head and say, 'Good morning, Paul,' and her hair will be black all over and she will greet me as if nothing has happened, nothing has changed. That is the strange thing about Paris.

I put my face to the gap in the window and smelled the bleach from below. Teresa was talking to her husband in Portuguese. He was standing around with the Sunday baguette tucked under his arm. Lucky bastard. I bet it was still warm. I could smell it on the wind.

I got my secret carton of Pringles out of the wardrobe and then I went back to my computer and I looked up more stuff. I read about an app for men who are looking for men who want sex. It's called *bander*, which means to have an erection in French. I opened the Pringles. You enter your location and a description of yourself and what you want and then a map comes up and there is a red circle that is you and there are green flashing circles near you and they are the men who want it as bad as you do.

I downloaded the app. I looked through all the photos men had posted of their torsos, six-packs without heads, faces with beards. I read about what they wanted to do, who they wanted to do it to. I had to look up what the abbreviations meant. One guy boasted he had straight men knocking down his door for sex and another guy said he was looking for tough love. Eric said he worked in retail at Charles de Gaulle, Terminal 2E, but he could do it in his lunch hour. He said he was big like you'd dreamed of.

And then Scarlett called.

'Why didn't you call me back?' she said. 'I was waiting for you. You don't know how bored I've been.'

She wanted to know what had happened, if I had

spoken to Max again. I said no and I asked her if she had heard of *bander*. She had, of course, she knew all about it, she'd read about it on the Internet or in a magazine, I can't remember how she knew, but she knew. She said the app came from America, that gay blokes love it because it means they can get sex anyplace, anytime. She sounded like an ad on the radio when she said that. She told me they were going to launch an app like that for heterosexuals.

A text came in from my father while I was on the phone. He was asking to see me, asking if I could come round. I must have gone silent because Scarlett said:

'Are you still there, Paul?'

'Yeah, I'm still here.'

'Talk to me, then.' Her voice was demanding, like a child's. But then her mum called out to her and she said she had to go, they were driving back to Paris. She said she'd see me tomorrow at school.

I wondered if she was still in love with Stéphane. She'd started wearing her skirts shorter and her jeans tighter for school and she left her shirts undone so that you could see what you wanted. She made out she was over him, but whenever I went to McDo's for lunch, as soon as I got back she always asked: 'Did you see him?'

I knew she tracked him on Facebook. Sometimes she'd be round at my apartment, lying on my bed, on her phone and she would shout out, 'Slut,' and I knew she was looking up Inès. She said Stéphane was only going out with Inès for her tits. But I reckoned what Stéphane really wanted from Inès was someone as beautiful as him, someone to add to his cool.

Sometime later on that afternoon, Gabriel came home. I heard him in the corridor first, and then he opened my bedroom door without knocking. I made the page on my screen go small.

'Hey, Paul,' he said. 'Long time no see. Is your mum about?'

He looked rough, like he hadn't slept for a week.

'She went out,' I said.

'Do you know where?'

'No.'

'OK, well, I'm back from the gig. We had a great crowd; they really loved us. You should come next time. Bring Scarlett with you, I'll get you tickets, I'll get you a backstage pass.'

I said nothing. I just stared at him and then I turned back to my computer.

'Oh, yeah, Paul, I know what I wanted to ask. I don't suppose you can lend me some cash, can you? I forgot to pick some up on the way home.'

'How much?' I was still facing my computer.

'How much you got?' I heard him step towards me. I shrugged and turned to look at him.

'A hundred.'

'Man, you're loaded. Where do you get all that cash from?'

'Same place you do,' I said.

He laughed. He looked a little guilty.

I swung back around and opened the drawer beneath my computer. I could feel him watching over my shoulder. I pulled out the cash. He reached out his hand to take the money.

'Thanks, mate, I'll pay you back.' He left my room, slipping the notes into his jeans pocket as he went, closing the door behind him. I turned to my screen again. A little later the intercom buzzer went. I knew Gabriel wouldn't get it and Cindy was still out, so I stood up to answer it, but by the time I opened my bedroom door, Gabriel was heading down the corridor towards the intercom. My bedroom was between him and the intercom and when he saw me in the doorway, I swear he picked up speed.

'I'll get that, Paul,' he said.

I shrugged. I turned to go back in my bedroom just as he picked up the receiver.

'Yeah, mate, yeah,' I heard him say. 'I'll be right down.'

He went out, leaving the apartment door ajar. I could hear him as he thumped his way downstairs. The television was on in the salon; he'd been watching some home-improvement show and there was a guy in a shiny black suit telling a woman she would never sell her house because her front garden looked like a municipal dump. The woman was standing on her doorstep sobbing.

'First impressions count, Sylvie,' the man was saying, 'and your garden makes me want to run away.'

I opened the windows in the salon and stepped up onto the balcony. This side of the apartment looks out onto the road. It was silent below; there was no one about, only parked cars. Nothing moved. The curling balustrades and the grey slate roofs pressed tight against me. I felt dizzy standing there looking down.

A figure moved in the shadows below. Someone was down there on the pavement outside our door. I leaned over, gripping the balcony rail. Someone was standing astride a moped. I thought perhaps Gabriel had ordered pizza. The guy below had a motorbike helmet on, but I couldn't see a pizza box.

The door to our apartment building opened and Gabriel stepped out. I heard him say hi as he reached into his pocket and pulled out my cash. The guy in the helmet counted the notes and then he pulled out an envelope from inside his jacket and handed it over. Then he revved his moped and drove back along the pavement towards the Rue d'Assas. I heard the door to the building close.

I came back in and closed the windows and walked back across the salon and stood at the entrance to it. A couple of minutes later Gabriel pushed open the front door. He had his head down and he was looking inside the envelope; his right hand was feeling around inside. He didn't see me standing there.

'What's that?' I said.

He jumped.

'Paul, man, you gave me a fright. Why do you creep up on me like that?'

'I didn't creep up on you, I was just standing here,' I said. 'What's in the envelope?'

'Just some stuff that I need, you know, for the band,

some documents and stuff to do with the tour. Did I tell you we're doing a tour? Man, that is a bad programme, that is,' he said, changing the subject and grabbing hold of the remote. He flicked across the channels for a couple of minutes and then he said:

'I gotta take a shower.'

He walked past me, the envelope tucked under his left arm. He went into maman's bedroom and shut the door behind him.

I went back into my bedroom and closed the door. Later, when I looked up from my screen, I saw the family opposite was having supper; it must have been 8 p.m. Maman still wasn't home. They were all sitting at their table. There were lamps in the room that made pools of light around their heads so they looked like a painting in a museum. I stood up and switched the light off in my bedroom. I sat back down on my bed.

They took ages eating. The mother was doing most of the talking. The father kept shutting his eyes and chewing. The light shone on his forehead. Every so often he poured himself a little wine. He dabbed at his mouth with a white napkin. The table was laid with a white tablecloth and there were silver pots for salt and pepper and a glass jug in the centre. I wondered what they were eating. The eldest daughter got up and left the room. She came back carrying a plate of cheese. I saw the chalk-white skin of the Brie – almost gleaming – and I could taste it in my mouth. There were five of them sitting around the table, each one of them alone.

Suddenly the girl with black hair stood up and turned so that she was facing me. She strode towards where I sat on the other side of the courtyard. She reached up her hand, grabbed hard at the red velvet curtain, and pulled the fabric across. She didn't look at me, even though I knew I was the cause of her anger: me watching her. She walked to the other curtain and she snatched and dragged until both curtains closed in a heavy screen of darkness and I was shut out, alone.

12

My father was waiting for me when I came out of school at lunchtime, waiting like he never waits for me.

'What are you doing here?' I asked.

He was wearing his suit and tie. Everyone was looking at us.

'I came to see you,' he said.

Scarlett was standing next to me; we'd said we'd go and get noodles together. She watched us both, her big red sunglasses stacked up on top of her head, her eyes going back and forth between my father and me.

'Aren't you going to introduce us, Paul?' She twirled a strand of hair around her finger, put her head to one side, and pushed her lips together to make them look sexy.

'This is Scarlett,' I said.

'Bonjour, monsieur.' She said it in a breathy kind of way, holding out her hand for him to shake, letting her jacket fall open so that you could see the words 'Born Wild' across her breasts.

'Hello,' my father said. He shook her hand. He didn't say anything else.

There was a moment of silence. I looked down at the pavement. And then Scarlett said:

'Well, I guess I should leave you guys together. I've got

to get lunch. See you later, Paul. Goodbye, monsieur.' She walked off down the road, but I saw her turn and check us out before she carried on along the Rue d'Assas.

'Is that your girlfriend?' my father said when she had gone a little way.

I didn't reply.

'She's not beautiful, but she's got something.'

'She's not my fucking girlfriend, all right?'

I'd never sworn at him before.

'It was just a question,' he said. But he didn't tell me off for talking to him like that.

We walked along the road in the direction of the Jardin du Luxembourg.

'I thought we could go out for lunch.'

I said nothing.

'Where do you normally go?'

'McDo's,' I said.

'Your mother'll kill me if we go there.'

'She lets me have the Big Mac menu,' I said.

'Yeah, well, you should know by now, Paul, your mother never plays by the rules.'

We walked on for a bit.

'How about we go get a crêpe instead?' he said.

A crêpe, my god; he hadn't bought me a crêpe in years. He hadn't even bought me a crêpe when he told me they were breaking up. All I got then was a quick walk to the jardin and back before he dumped me at the apartment with the removal men. We crossed over Rue Guynemer. My thighs were shaking.

'So,' he said. 'How have you been?'

I shrugged.

'I texted you, but you didn't reply.'

I didn't say anything.

'Why didn't you reply, Paul?' We were walking side by side, looking straight ahead.

'I didn't have anything to say.'

'I was worried.'

Pierre and Guillaume were just ahead of us on their way to McDo's. I saw them turn and stare.

'How's school?' he said.

When I didn't reply he asked:

'Have you had any results?'

I wasn't playing that game any more.

'Nope,' I said.

'Do you want to tell me what this is about, Paul?'

'What what is about?'

He looked across at me then and I stared back. I saw his pupils dilate, ink spots growing large. It was him that said nothing this time. We walked through the open gates and into the jardin. There was no sunlight, only grey in the December sky, grey in the faces of the people who walked in the cold under the bare trees. We walked between the muddied lawns, past the miniature Statue of Liberty. The trees were wet and stained black. Their branches had been cut back, brutalized, leaving only stumps. A pack of guys from the lycée were standing there, shouting and pushing each other. They looked up as I passed by with my dad in his suit.

I saw my father's feet walking alongside mine on the gravel that was wet and brown and covered in dead stalks from the trees. I saw his hand in his trouser pocket and I wanted to smack him to the ground. I wanted to punch him in the stomach, smack him in the six-pack that he'd spent so long sculpting. I wanted to stamp on him, stamp on his face, stamp on his bollocks, make him bleed. Make him cry. I wanted him to know how much I hated him.

'How was your race?' I said. My voice came out uneven.

'Which one?'

'The one you did last weekend. Remember?'

'Oh, yeah, I had to pull out. Shin splints. They hurt like hell and if you don't rest they get worse. Todd said I shouldn't risk it. I don't want to tear myself up before Puerto Rico next spring. Todd says I've got to rest up now, I've got to listen to my body.'

'Todd.' I smiled, but not a nice smile, a twisted smile, a smile to make my father sweat. 'Your animal man.'

'My what?'

'You know,' I said, 'your animal man.'

'What does that mean?' He looked uncomfortable.

'Nothing. It means nothing. Does it? So what did you do?' I said.

'To my shins?'

'No, last weekend, what did you do?'

'Not much. Bit of strength training. I had a lot of work to do. I'm working on a deal.'

'I bet,' I said.

We walked the last few metres in silence, past the ground where they were playing pétanque. There were mostly old guys out playing; Teresa's husband was there. I heard the clicking of the metal in their hands and the smack as the boule hit the wooden barrier. I could smell the crêpes. A lady was making them in the kiosk, standing behind the counter underneath a trail of plastic sunflowers, pouring the beige liquid onto the griddle in front of her. Her eyes lit up when she saw my father.

'Hello, monsieur, young man, what can I get you?'

'I'll try your soup of the day,' my father said.

'I do the croûtons myself.' She tucked a wisp of her hair behind her ear as if she were a girl. 'Thierry,' she shouted to a toothless old guy hanging round the side of the kiosk, 'run and get me some bread!' Then she smiled at me. 'You look like you could do with one of my famous crêpes.'

There were pictures of cows all over the kiosk; post-cards and fridge magnets, plastic cows hanging from the ceiling, black-and-white cows with huge pink swollen udders. Her breasts were pushed together under a shiny green python-print top and when she bent down to put the milk away, her satin trousers stretched tight across her arse. She picked up the whisk and started beating the crêpe mixture. My dad and I went and sat down at a small metal table. We sat in silence for a bit, me looking at my phone, my dad looking at his. After a while he looked up at me and said:

'Are you angry about something, Paul?'

I thought, if I open my mouth now, it will come out,

my liquid rage, it will pour out like lava onto the table, it will melt the white plastic goblets; it will drip down onto my father's handmade leather shoes.

'Is it the divorce, Paul? Are you angry about the divorce?'

I couldn't speak for a few seconds. I bit the inside of my mouth until I tasted blood and then it started.

'Is that what you always do? Get a man in a black hood? Is that, like, your special request? Because I know that's what you all have, your "special requests".'

'What are you talking about, Paul?' His face was pale.

'You. I'm talking about you. Being fucked by a man with a big head and no hair. Remember?'

There was no iris left to his eyes, only guilt.

'I don't know what you are talking about.'

'Oh yes, you do, you fucking do. The laundry room, remember? I saw you. I was there.'

I must have shouted that because the lady sitting across from us looked around. I saw her perk up at the sound of a fight. My father said nothing. We waited; my breath was coming in big gusts.

'Voilà, monsieur.' The crêpe lady leaned across my father to put down his soup, pushing her python-print tits as close to him as she dared. 'And a Nutella crêpe and a Coke for you, my love.' She cocked her head expectantly. My father looked like he was dying. She waited for him to smile and then she headed back to her kiosk.

He checked to make sure the woman next to us wasn't listening and then he said,

'What did you see?'

'What do you think I saw? Him hammering you in the laundry room. Sweat all over you.'

'How did you get in?'

'Essie.'

'Essie?'

'She gave me keys. She said I might need them. I was down in the park and I saw your light was on and it looked warm and I was cold and I was on my own. You told me you were at a race. I thought I could go up and be in your apartment, hang out, even if you weren't there; maybe I could wait for you. I could surprise you, be there when you got home.'

He didn't say anything for a bit. He just sat there staring at the table with his face creased up like he was in pain. And then he looked up at me and said:

'It was an accident, Paul. I got onto some site by mistake. I don't know what happened. I was looking for bike stuff. I was looking for biking kit for a race. And then I thought I'd do it once. I don't know why. I can't explain, I thought . . . I don't know what I thought. It just happened. I don't expect you to understand. I don't even understand myself.'

'Who was he?'

He put his head in his hands.

'I'm not gay if that is what you are thinking.'

'Is that why you left us? Because you're gay?'

'I said I'm not gay, Paul. I told you. I'm not gay. You have to believe me. It was an accident. I wanted to stop. I will stop.'

'You mean you've done it before?'

'No. No. I have not done it before. I didn't say that.'

'You just said you wanted to stop and now you will stop.'

'I haven't done it before.'

'What about the text in the car?'

'What text?' He looked confused.

'The text when we came back from your parents. "Come back, big boy. I'm gonna treat you mean." That fucking text.'

'That was a woman,' he said. But he was lying.

I took a bite of my crêpe. I was crying. He sat with his head bowed and I took great big flabby bites of crêpe, one after the other, stuffing it into me so that it grew inside my mouth like that yellow stuff they give you at the orthodontist when they are fitting you for a brace; it swelled inside me, choked me with its sweet and sagging pulp.

After a while he looked up and said:

'Have you told your mother?'

My mouth was full. I shook my head.

'It's just that our case is heard soon. We go in front of the judge . . .' He paused. He moved his hands through the air and then he said:

'I'm just trying to say the divorce has taken so long, it would be difficult if you told her now, it would delay things and we are trying to close the – ' he searched around for a word other than deal – 'we are trying to close the divorce.'

I swallowed all the crêpe that was in my mouth.

'Is that all you care about?' I said.

'Listen, Paul, I understand you are angry—' he started, but I cut him off.

'What if I close my eyes at night and I see you and that guy? What does that make me? You keep saying, "I'm not gay, I'm not gay," but I heard you, you were begging for it. I know all about what goes on, all those straight guys who just want to get shafted. I've read about it. You told me I shouldn't lie, you went on and on at me about my marks, always my marks, that they aren't good enough for your son. You know what? That seventeen, you were right, I cheated. I looked at Guillaume's paper and I let him use my PSP so that he would let me cheat. But you, you lied to all of us, to maman, to your parents, to me, you lied to me. Everything about you is a lie, you are one big fucking lie.'

'It's not what you think. It was something I did, something I did to see if I could feel. I was trying to reach oblivion. You see, I am damaged, Paul. Do you know what an abyss is? Do you know what I mean by that? All that I have striven for, all that I have worked for, and I am in the dark hole of an abyss.'

I cried out then.

'I don't care about you. I don't care about your abyss. It's always about you. You, you, you. What about me? It's in my head now and I can't get it out. You kept it from me, you hid it away all this time so that I had to go searching for it, searching and scrabbling around in the shit until I found the truth.'

'This is not the truth, Paul.'

'Don't fucking tell me what the truth is. I saw you.'

'You don't understand. It's not what you think you saw.'

I stood up to go.

'Don't you ever think about me?' I said.

I had Nutella smeared all over my fingers and there were tears and crap from my nose running down my face.

'I wanted you to care about me.' I was sobbing.

'I do care,' he said.

'No, you don't!' I shouted. 'It's you that you care about. It always has been.'

'Paul, listen to me.' He stood up, knocking the table, upsetting my glass of Coke. The dark liquid spilled across the table, spreading out across the white paper tablecloth, blistering the paper before dripping to the ground. There was fear in his eyes, but even that was for himself. Feeling sorry for himself, scared I would tell maman, scared I would blow the divorce proceedings sky-high, wondering how he could make the situation go away.

'When you broke up you promised me it would be better,' I said. 'You said it would be better for me if you were apart, that you wouldn't fight all the time. You said it here. Right here in this jardin. You said I would be happier.'

'Yes,' he said, 'I said that.'

They were all looking at us now, the woman sitting next to us, the crêpe lady, Thierry the toothless guy, the Japanese teenage girls, all looking at the fat boy shouting at his dad, wondering what the problem was, why he was crying, why his world was falling apart.

'I am not happy,' I said.

'I know that, Paul. I know you're not.'

'I am not happy because of you.' I jabbed my finger at him. I couldn't hold it in. I couldn't control it. I ran at my father. I punched his chest with a closed fist.

'You!' I shouted. 'What have you done to me?'

I went to punch him again, but he held back my hand.

'Stop, Paul. Don't do this.'

'You lied!' I shouted. 'You lied to me.' And then I turned and ran from him. I heard him calling out my name as I ran past the guys playing pétanque; I heard their laughter. I ran past Teresa's husband polishing his boule with a piece of cloth, past the empty hangers on the metal coat stand and the pile of dead leaves rotting inside the cage. I ran out of the big black gates and I ran across Rue Guynemer. I looked back, but he wasn't following me.

I turned onto Rue d'Assas. I was out of breath. I put my hands on my knees, leaned my head over a bin and stood there, listening to my sobs. Then I shoved my fingers to the back of my throat and I kept them there until all the crêpe surged up and out of me, into the bin. I didn't care who saw me. I retched it out.

I wiped my mouth with the back of my hand. I caught my breath. I tried to stop the sobbing. I cleared the crêpe out of my nose; I snorted it onto the pavement. I used the front of my sweatshirt to wipe away the tears and the saliva. Then I waited for the number 82 bus to go past me and I ran out across the road. I ran until I reached school and then I went inside to find Scarlett.

13

After school Scarlett came back to my apartment. I was glad she was there. She lay on my bed with her legs in a diamond shape and I could see the crotch of her bleached jeans.

'What did your dad want?' she asked.

'I don't know.'

'He doesn't say much,' she said.

I was staring out the window, watching the guy who lives opposite on the floor below. He was sitting in front of his computer. His head was at a strange angle to his neck, kind of locked forward and down, as if he wanted to fit his whole head inside the screen.

'Does he have a girlfriend?' Scarlett said.

I wondered what it is that makes us look and look, what we think we'll find inside our screens.

'Paul?' she said.

I turned around.

'Are you OK?'

She was staring at me. She looked different. Tender. Like a flower.

'Yeah,' I said. 'I'm OK.'

She watched me for a few seconds as if she was trying

to figure something out and then she suddenly jumped off my bed.

'I forgot,' she said. 'I've got something for you.'

She felt around inside the back pocket of her jeans and then she reached out her hand and opened it. There was a gold medallion lying there. I stood up and took it from Scarlett. It was warm in my hand. We were standing close, Scarlett and I. It was dark outside and only my bedside light was lit. She was barefoot and staring at me, but softly staring.

'It's the miraculous medallion, Paul, remember?' She said it in a kind of whisper. 'Saint Catherine gave them out when there was a cholera epidemic and all these people who were dying were miraculously saved. Thousands of them. I got it at the shop at the Chapel.'

'Thanks,' I said, 'I like it.'

'It's not real gold or anything.'

There was a picture of the Virgin Mary and the light pouring out of her hands, like the sculpture at the Chapel. I turned it over. On the other side there was a cross entwined with the letter M. And there were stars going all the way around and at the bottom there were two hearts, side by side, one with a crown of thorns around it, the other pierced through by a sword.

'That's us, Paul,' Scarlett said. 'You and me. Two wounded hearts. No matter what they do to you, you still keep wanting them to love you. And then you hate yourself for thinking that way.'

I looked up; she was smiling but she had tears in her eyes. It was like she knew without me telling her. It was like she understood. I thought about telling her about my father, thought about letting her in. I tried to think what I would say. But I couldn't do it.

We stood for a minute without saying anything, just staring at each other with our hands by our sides, and then her phone made a noise and she looked down at it and the moment was gone. I didn't know how to get it back.

She said she wanted to get a glass of water. I checked my phone. I had heard nothing from my father since lunchtime. Scarlett was gone for a long time. I went out in the corridor to see where she was. The door to maman's bedroom was open when I went by. Something moved and caught my eye. Scarlett was just coming out of maman's dressing room. She turned and closed the door behind her, quietly, so that no one would hear. She looked up and saw me watching her.

'Your mum's got some amazing clothes.' Swiftly, lightly, she spoke, as if she wanted to talk before I could, as if she wanted to make the fact that she was walking out of my mother's dressing room seem like nothing.

'What are you doing?' I said. I was cold inside.

'Just checking out her stuff. She's got such beautiful stuff, god, I love her shoes. She's got so many. I wish my mum dressed like her.'

'I thought you were getting a glass of water,' I said.

'I am.'

She walked past where I was standing in the doorway and down the corridor and into the kitchen where Cindy was feeding Lou.

'Hello, Lou, my beautiful baby. How's she doing, Cindy? Still no solids?' She spoke loudly, too loudly. She asked about Lou's reflux, about when Cindy would start her on purées. She talked quickly, asking questions, scarcely waiting for a reply. She wouldn't draw breath. I stood in the doorway. When at last she ran out of questions, she turned to me and said:

'What are you looking at, Paul?'

'You,' I said.

She held my gaze. Her phone beeped with a message. She looked down.

'I gotta go,' she said, but then she took forever leaving, getting her bag, putting her boots back on, saying goodbye to Lou; it was like she was treading water, waiting for something to happen or for me to say something. But I didn't.

After she'd gone, I sat back at my computer. I stayed there until the smell of frying brought me out of my room.

Cindy was cooking spring rolls in the kitchen. She'd been to Chinatown to buy the ingredients. She takes the number 83 bus there with her wheelie trolley. I went with her once. She meets friends in the supermarket; they go up and down the aisles filling their trolleys with bags of frozen shredded pork, bunches of spring onions that smell on the bus on the way home, and strange flat fish with ugly dead eyes that Cindy says are Philippine fish. When

I went with her, she took me to a little shop that sold only Philippine stuff and she ran her fingers along the shelves until she found her favourite cookies. She had tears in her eyes when she took them off the shelf. She said they were her children's favourite. We ate them on the bus on the way home; they tasted of peanuts and washing-up liquid, but I didn't tell her that.

When she gets back from the market, she goes upstairs to her room and spends hours cutting up carrots into tiny batons and slicing the spring onions. She lays them with the mangetouts in piles on the chopping board. Then she takes squares of pastry and arranges the filling at one end of each and rolls the pastry over and over, her fingers pushing and tucking until she has made a sausage shape that she seals at the end like an envelope. The fat ones are vegetarian; the small skinny ones are pork. She makes tons, a hundred or more, and she wraps them in foil so they are silver pads of ridges and furrows.

The first time I tasted Cindy's spring rolls was during that massive heat wave when all those old people died in Paris, baked alive in their apartments. I sat on Cindy's bed under the burning roof; the air smelled of the shared toilet out on the corridor and shopping bags full of rubbish that people hang outside their doors. The heat pulsed off the ceiling onto her forehead so her face was sweating, but she smiled as she fried the spring rolls in boiling oil. Her room is so small she has her shower next to her stove. I waited as the black smoke filled my mouth and the room and made my eyes water.

I could smell them now from down the corridor. Little spurts of saliva gathered in my mouth. Maman was away for the day in Milan. Cindy cooks spring rolls in the apartment only when maman is away, because maman can't stand the smell of deep-fat frying. I love that smell.

I went into the kitchen and stood next to Cindy and I watched as the spring rolls turned dark and crispy. I waited as she laid them out one by one on a bed of white kitchen roll. I ate them in the kitchen, just Cindy and me; she'd put Lou to bed by then. I dipped each one in sticky chilli sauce until they were glossy and red. There was no one to stop me. I ate one after the other, the strands of grey pork falling on my chin as I sucked at my fingers, licked the oil from around my mouth.

Don't think it went away. It was there as I gorged myself, there whenever I woke up, whatever time it was, there when I sat in lessons with my arm outstretched along the hot radiator, staring down at the empty courtyard below. It was there all the time; a great dark lump lodged in my heart, and it grew bigger every day, until it took up all my chest, until the burning anger of it made me feel sick even as I stuffed my face with Cindy's spring rolls.

Maman messaged me to say her plane was delayed and she still hadn't left Milan. 'I've bought you a pair of black Nikes, Paul. You're gonna love them.' When I was little she used to bring me back a stuffed toy whenever she went away. At one time I had a hundred and twenty-two stuffed toys on my bed. Then she started buying me clothes, trying to style me: skinny jeans, hoodies, T-shirts with English words on, the kind of kit Stéphane wears. I've got wardrobes of the stuff, but most of it doesn't fit me. That's why she buys me shoes now.

Five minutes after maman's text, I got one from my father.

'Are you there, Paul?' he said.

I didn't reply.

I woke up in the night with a start. I'd dreamed Lou was in my bed, I'd dreamed I had rolled over and crushed her and she was dead, squashed beneath my shoulder, beige and lifeless, like an uncooked spring roll. I checked my phone; it was 1:48 a.m. I was sweating. Scarlett had sent a video of a monkey in a zoo in India. It was clinging to its cage, its fingers rattling the bars, trying to escape, its mouth open in a scream.

'Let me out,' Scarlett wrote.

My breath was coming too fast. I thought of Scarlett and the two hearts; I thought of her coming out of my mother's dressing room. I thought of my father. I got out of bed to check on Lou. I opened my bedroom door. Somewhere in the apartment, maman and Gabriel were arguing. I stood for a moment listening to their voices, remembering when maman and my father used to argue. Just like old times.

'You do nothing,' maman said.

They were in the kitchen, one on either side of the island, like when maman had the fight with my grandmother. The big white light that hangs from the ceiling lit up their faces. Maman still had her coat on; she was leaning forward across the island, her face pale, her eyes bloodshot from the plane. Gabriel was standing where my grandmother had stood.

'You do nothing all day and meanwhile I'm flying to Milan and back working to pay for all this.' She swept her hand through the air across the beige marble of the kitchen island.

'I'm back now, babe. I can help.'

'You can't even get yourself dressed.'

'I've been under a lot of pressure recently with the band, you know, and the tour. I just need some time to unwind.'

'Oh my god, Gabriel, you are not Mick Jagger. You played five gigs as a support band. Don't talk to me about pressure. It's me that's working, that's travelling, that's paying the bills. You've got no responsibilities. You just hang out with your friends, drink some beers, eat my food, and sleep in my bed, and Cindy washes your clothes. I'm paying for this, you know. I pay for everything about you, your drugs, your beers, your baby, it's me that pays.'

She was like a woodpecker banging away at him. I saw one once in the Jardin du Luxembourg a long time ago. I heard it first and then I saw its olive-green back, a red flash at its head. I saw it hammering its beak against a trunk, splinters of bark flying off. But woodpeckers have special padding around their brains so they don't get hurt.

'It's tough for me, babe. You've done it all before. This is my first time. I don't know what to do. I mean, you know about routines and stuff like that and I don't know anything about milk and car seats. Come on, babe.' He walked around the island towards my mother. 'Take it easy on me,' he said.

'Don't screw me around, Gabriel,' maman said. But she didn't sound angry any more; she sounded scared.

He reached out and started to undo the belt around her coat, pulling her to him as he did.

'Babe, I'm right here,' he said.

'Don't mess with my head, Gabriel. I can't take any more.'

He put his hand at the back of her neck and drew her to him. They kissed until he pulled his mouth away from my mother's mouth and said, 'Hey, I got something good for us to share.'

Maman turned then and saw me standing in the corridor. She gave a kind of jump.

'Why do you do that, Paul? Why do you creep up on us like that?'

'You woke me up,' I said.

'I hate it when you do that.'

It was happening right in front of me. Something was draining from her – her looks, her power? I've seen her stare and stare in the mirror, like she can't get enough, like she's drinking from her own beauty. That's why she always smiles in photos, because she's smiling at herself. Did she think it would last for ever?

'Go back to bed, Paul.' Her voice was sad. I wondered

if she was ill, if it was an illness that was doing this to her.

Then Lou let out a sudden cry that burst from the baby monitor on the island, bleak and insistent.

'She does it every time!' maman shouted, slamming her fist down on the counter. 'I've told her not to leave it on full volume. I said go to bed, Paul. I can't cope with you as well.'

14

Maman said she wanted to go to Megève for Christmas. She said Estelle was planning on going with Max, that they were renting a chalet at Mont d'Arbois and we should go with them.

'Wouldn't that be cosy, Paul? Wrapped up and drinking hot chocolate on Christmas Day? Fun, no?'

I would have liked to see the crystal mountains in the sun, to watch the slabs of snow fall from the roofs and smash to the ground, powder at my feet. But I wasn't sure Megève was a real plan. I wondered if it was just another of her whims, one that she discusses with everyone – me, Gabriel, Estelle, not her mother because they still weren't talking, but her hairdresser, her clients, her assistant at work – obsessing about how to get there, which restaurants to book, who else was going, what to wear, which bar to try, only for it all to burst like a bubble and leave no trace.

I couldn't figure out what she would do next, what was real and what was not. One moment she was sobbing because a client cancelled a shoot that left her right down on her end-of-year targets, then in her next breath, she'd be on the phone ordering a sofa from Milan that cost ten thousand euros. She came home from work the day the sofa arrived and saw Gabriel with his feet up on it and she let out a scream. But the next night I found them lying together on the sofa, Gabriel with his feet up and maman smoking a cigarette, quiet as a lamb.

Catalogues showing pictures of couples sitting in front of open fires and snow falling outside kept arriving for maman. Guys at school were talking about what they were going to get for Christmas. Cindy went shopping on the Champs-Élysées and bought a big blue-and-silver Cinderella dress for her daughter and a Paris Saint-Germain football kit for her son.

My dad messaged asking when he could see me at Christmas. I hadn't seen him since the Jardin du Luxembourg. I blew him out the weekend I was supposed to go to his place. Maman didn't ask me why I didn't want to go; she said it was up to me what I did.

I sat in my bedroom after school, checking out Scarlett's Facebook page. I scrolled through everything of hers, the music videos, the rap, the anti-animal-cruelty stuff, a video of a sheep getting manhandled on its way to becoming an Ugg boot. I went through pictures of all her friends. I looked at the photos of her and Stéphane when they were together, kissing for the camera, tongues touching, Stéphane with one eye fixed on me like he knew I was watching. I wanted to tell him that Scarlett was mine now.

'Are you there?' I wrote.

My phone rang straightaway. I thought it was Scarlett, but it was my grandmother. She never calls me. She wanted to know if I would be at their Christmas Eve dinner; she said my father had said he still didn't know and so she'd decided to find out for herself. Christmas Eve in Neuilly. I could smell it. My grandmother says the scent is her Christmas tree from Normandy, but maman told me once it's really just a scented candle my grandmother hides behind the clock on the mantelpiece.

It used to be fun when maman was there; she always gave over-the-top, expensive gifts, like the latest remote-control helicopter or an iPod for my cousins or a Gucci handbag for my grandmother. The cousins tore into her presents first while my aunt and grandmother sat rolling their eyes in disapproval, making faces across the ripped wrapping paper. I remember one year maman gave Catherine a red satin Dior nightdress. It made Catherine blush when she opened it and her hands shook so that it slid from the silk tissue paper onto the floor. Christmas presents were maman's way of reminding them she wouldn't play by their rules.

'She drives me crazy,' my grandmother was saying. 'Making your father wait and wait until the very last moment to tell him when he can have you. It's all part of her game.'

'Why does he want me now?' I said. 'He never wanted me before.'

She should have listened to me then, she should have stopped and heard the tremor in my voice, but she laughed instead, her chandelier laugh.

'What an extraordinary thing to say,' she said.

It was her laughter that made it leap out of me.

'I'm not coming to your Christmas Eve. I don't want to see him. I don't want to see you. I'm sick of it. Him, you, your whole existence, all your puffed-up hair, your gold digicode and your assisted parking because you can't even park a fucking car.'

'You can't speak—' she started to say, but I ran her over.

'You blame her for everything, you think she's not good enough, but she's better than the whole lot of you. Ask him why I won't come for Christmas. Ask your son. He knows why. Ask him why I don't ever want to see him again.'

I had more to say, but she wouldn't listen. The line was dead.

I didn't feel regret. I felt triumph. I wanted to climb out onto the balustrade and shout so that the girl opposite would look up from her books and see me and she would laugh and punch the air. I wanted to ring maman and tell her what I had done, tell her that I had said what she had always wanted to say, that I had defended her.

'My prince,' she would say. 'I love you too much.'

I called her on her mobile, but she didn't pick up. I called her again straight away, but she didn't answer. And then I remembered she was in London, which meant she'd be in a meeting or at some kind of appointment. I didn't leave a message. I thought of calling Scarlett, but she hadn't replied to my message. And then I remembered her face as she came out of maman's dressing room.

The adrenalin drained out of me as quickly as it had come. It left me hollow. It left me hungry. I stood at my bedroom window looking out. It was one of those December days when the sun never comes out; all day long the sky was a band of dark cloud that pressed down low over the courtyard. Everything about that day was waiting for darkness. The cobbles below were wet and slippery. Stay away from the window, Paul. Go find Cindy.

The next day I waited for Scarlett at the lockers where we usually meet to go and get lunch, but she didn't turn up. I messaged her, but she didn't reply. I wondered if she was with Stéphane. I didn't see her all that day. The next morning was Wednesday and I hung out in the corridor before geography, standing by the windows, looking down into the courtyard to see if she was below.

I looked up; she was coming towards me.

'Hi, Paul,' she said, but she didn't stop walking.

'Looking hot today,' a guy in my class shouted after her.

She turned and laughed. Her mouth was painted a burning red. I'd never seen her lips that colour.

I sat through geography wondering why she didn't stop to talk, why she didn't message me back. I wondered if she would come and find me for lunch, but she didn't. I looked for her on the Rue Vavin, but she wasn't at the noodle bar or at the bakery. She wasn't in the jardin.

I walked up and down the paths; I looked for her on the benches over by the bandstand. I walked to the other side of the circular basin and back.

I didn't see her all afternoon, but at the end of lessons she was there, waiting for me at my locker, as if everything was normal and nothing had changed. She was texting when I walked up, but she put her phone away when she saw me. She asked if she could come back to my place.

She linked arms with me on the Rue d'Assas and told me that she'd missed me. I wanted to believe her; the warmth of her body felt good next to mine as we walked together down the road. When I asked her why she hadn't replied to any of my messages, she said she'd been too busy. I asked her if she was back with Stéphane.

'I've left him behind,' she said and she laughed out loud.

She told me she got three in a chemistry test and four in a maths test and that the school had contacted her parents and she was in trouble. She said her parents had grounded her and that's why she hadn't come around after school the past two nights. I asked her why she wasn't going straight home now and she said:

'Are you checking up on me, Paul?'

She told me her parents were making her do extra work at home, that she was exhausted from all the work. But she didn't look exhausted; she looked as if someone had set fire to her from the inside. She didn't stop fidgeting as we walked along and when we turned onto my road, she stopped and got her phone out again. She pretended she was checking her texts, but I saw her using the screen as a mirror, swooshing up her hair to make herself look hot, piling it high like a bird's nest. She pressed her lips together and pouted at herself.

All the way up in the lift to our apartment she talked nonstop, telling a story about what some guy had said in maths, speaking loudly, giggling as if it were hysterically funny, twisting a strand of hair around her fingers. She was still talking when she walked into my apartment, showing off as if there were an audience. I wondered if she'd been drinking. She broke off from her story and looked into the salon.

'Is anyone home?' she said.

I wondered who she meant by anyone.

We found Cindy in the kitchen feeding Lou. They both looked up when we walked in. Lou made funny noises like a dolphin and banged hard on the tray of her high chair. She had saliva running down both sides of her mouth. Her cheeks were red and her eyes were watering. She kept shaking her head and crying out.

'Poor baby has her first tooth,' Cindy said. 'She's been crying all day.'

Scarlett went over to Lou in her high chair. There was a little white chip of tooth pushing through Lou's top gum.

'Come to Scarlett,' she said. She hoisted Lou up into her arms then onto her hip. She held Lou close to her. 'I wish you were mine,' she said, resting her face in Lou's hair. 'I wish I could start all over again.'

I didn't know what she meant by that, but Lou smiled as if she understood. She thrust herself against Scarlett's waist with her legs wrapped around her; she grabbed at the necklace at Scarlett's throat and tried to slide her fingers beneath her T-shirt.

'Well, hello, stranger,' a voice said behind me.

It was Gabriel. He was standing barefoot in the doorway. He had his guitar slung around his neck and he was wearing his rock-star shirt, a red checked shirt with the sleeves ripped off to show us his biceps.

'Is that what you wear to school every day?' he said to Scarlett. 'My god, Paul, how do you get any work done?'

Scarlett blushed and pulled at her skirt. I said nothing.

'So, are you ready?' he said.

'Sure,' Scarlett said.

'Ready for what?' I said.

I looked across at Cindy. I saw the dark silence of her eyes. Scarlett went to hand Lou back to Cindy, but Lou didn't want to go back; she grabbed a handful of Scarlett's hair from the pile on top of her head and pulled. Scarlett squealed.

'Stop that, Lou,' she said, giggling, but Lou wouldn't let go; she kept tugging hard until Scarlett cried out in pain. 'Let me go, Lou,' she said. 'I have to go now.'

Cindy tried to prise Lou's fingers open and when she finally did, Lou screamed and beat her tiny fists against Cindy's shoulder. Cindy carried her away, out of the kitchen, down the corridor to her bedroom.

Gabriel looked at me and grinned.

'We're gonna make music,' he said.

Scarlett said nothing; she didn't look at me. She followed Gabriel out of the kitchen like she was pulled along on a string, walking away down the corridor, leaving me on my own.

I could hear Lou's screams from her bedroom, the same note, over and over, a dismal cry that vibrated in the back of her throat so that she sounded like an animal.

I stood for a few seconds with my hands rolled up in fists hanging down by my sides until the pain became too much. I pulled open the cupboard door; the rack slid open without a sound. There were racks of expensive nothing – chickpeas, brown rice, pasta, quinoa – stuff that could do nothing for me. At the back of the top rack I found a box of mini-chocolate biscuits meant for five-year-olds. Maman lets Cindy buy them because she reckons the smaller the biscuit, the less weight I'll put on. I ripped open the cardboard. I tore open each pack with my teeth and I held them above me and let each happy chocolate face fall into my mouth. I ate them five at a time. I ate them fast to get the factory-sweet creaminess, biscuits turning to mush against the roof of my mouth; I held it there, closing my eyes, the vacuum-packed vanilla in my nose, on my tongue, then I let the mush slide down the back of my throat and reload.

I found a packet of madeleines in the cupboard above the oven. I hate madeleines. I was crying as I licked the powdery crumbs from my hands and stuffed each dry sponge shell into my parched mouth. I was trying to reach oblivion; isn't that what my father said?

I opened the fridge door. A pale green oblong box was hiding behind the natural yoghurt. My heart leaped. I lifted the lid and the air sucked backwards and the scent of macaroons grabbed me and pulled me in. I ripped off the pad of paper, and there they were: coffee, salted caramel, chocolate, strawberry, raspberry, all those I love, waiting for me. I ate them. Twenty-four of them. Even the flavours I hate – rose, liquorice, violet – I ate them too. I threw them into my mouth. I pushed at them with my fingers, forcing them in to fill the emptiness.

I walked out to the corridor. I could hear them together. I didn't know she could sing. I didn't know her voice was soft and sad. I thought she was mine. It hurt so much. I needed to get the hurt out, to reach inside of me and rip it out with my own fingers if I had to. I ran to make it to the bathroom. I stood with my head above the toilet and I retched until there was nothing left. I stood and panted. I flushed the handle and washed the toilet with the brush. I'd read on the Internet what to do to keep them from finding out. I had madeleine crumbs in my underpants. I brushed my teeth and rinsed my mouth with mouthwash. The lights around the mirror made my face look green. There were tiny purple dots under the skin around my eyes.

I walked back along the corridor until I could see them. Gabriel was sitting across from her in a chair, head down, strumming on his guitar. They didn't look up. She was curled up on the sofa. She looked different when she was singing. Her eyes were half-closed so that I could see the pinkish flesh of her eyelids, and her mouth was round and sweet as she sang. She had taken off her shoes and her black-stockinged legs were tucked beneath her, her feet under her arse. Her T-shirt was sliding off one shoulder.

I wanted to strike her then. I wanted to hurt her. I wanted to tell her that she'd put on weight, that her thighs were fat, that Inès was hotter than her, that all the boys at school said so. I wanted to be Stéphane; he would know what to say to bring her back to his side. But I was me. I stood in the corridor outside the salon, watching them, too scared of losing her to say anything.

There was nowhere for me to go. The jardin was closed and it was dark outside. So I went back into my bedroom. I lay down on my bed and I waited for it to be over.

15

They sent us home from school early because the heating had broken down. I couldn't see Scarlett anywhere so I went to McDo's with Guillaume and Pierre instead. We walked back through the Jardin du Luxembourg. The crêpe lady was closed, her kiosk boarded up. They had taken away the huge piles of leaves from the metal cages. The jardin was bare without them. Someone had covered the carousel in yellow tarpaulin and it was caught up over the head of one of the wooden horses. Its eyes were missing; it stared at me from hollow black sockets. There was bird shit on the benches, and the flowers in the round beds were sodden and rotting on their stems.

We sat down on the sloping metal chairs to stuff our faces and drink Fanta. We sat by the weird fruit trees that they keep behind cages. The gardeners strap their branches to posts, tie up their limbs, stick plastic bags over their heads. Guillaume and Pierre were swapping porn on their phones, listening to music at the same time. Guillaume looked up from his screen and flicked his head in my direction.

'Hey, Paul,' he said. 'Where's your girlfriend?'

'Yeah, where's the hot babe?' Pierre said. 'Has she dumped you? Is that why you're hanging out with us?'

'She's not my girlfriend,' I said. I was already at the bottom of my fries. I should have ordered an extra portion.

'She's not your girlfriend?' Guillaume acted like he couldn't believe it; he looked over to Pierre and then back at me. 'What are you, gay or what?'

'He must be if he hasn't had Scarlett. She's desperate. Stéphane says she sends him pictures and videos of herself every day.'

'She does not,' I said.

'Wanna bet? I've seen them myself, videos of her touching herself and stuff, she sends them all the time, in the middle of the night. He told me.'

'He's a liar,' I said. I thought of the videos Scarlett sent me in the middle of the night, dolphins choking on plastic bags, guys out torching cars on the street. I thought of the videos I'd watched after I found my father in the laundry room. Guillaume reached into his box of fries.

'They're cold,' he said. 'I fucking hate cold fries.'

'She's a slut and everyone knows it,' Pierre said. His mouth was full of burger.

'Don't call her that,' I said.

He leaned back on his metal chair. He took another bite from his quarter-pounder.

'What you gonna do about it, gay boy?' Ketchup was oozing from the corner of his mouth.

Guillaume laughed. 'Hey, give him a break. It's not his fault he's gay.'

'I'm gonna put that on Facebook,' Pierre said. 'Paul is the only guy never to have had Scarlett.'

I stood up. My burger and the last of my fries fell to the ground.

'Wa-wa-wa-wa.' Pierre made a noise like a siren. He shouted over to Guillaume, 'Gay-boy alert!'

I charged at him then. I put both my hands on his shoulders and I shoved him hard and his chair fell over backwards. His eyes stretched wide as the chair hit the low metal hoops at the edge of the lawn and the back of his head hit the metal of the chair. We fell to the ground. I was on top of him. I smelled the meat and the gherkins swilling around inside his mouth. I hit him below the cheekbone, in the fleshy part of his face. It felt good. I felt strong. He was swearing at me and trying to shove me off him. I hit him again.

Pierre let out a high-pitched scream.

'I'm bleeding, fuck, I'm bleeding!'

Guillaume was pulling at my jacket, shouting at me to stop. I didn't want to stop. I wanted to smack him until he stopped moving.

'Get off him, Paul,' Guillaume shouted; he tried to grab my arm.

He pulled at my collar, dragging at it, trying to haul me off Pierre.

'You fucking arsehole,' I said to Pierre. I put my hand on his neck and shoved him again. 'Don't call me gay.'

I rolled off him. I got to my knees and then to my feet, trying to catch my breath. Pierre lay on his back whimpering and clutching at the side of his face. His burger lay on the ground, his yellow fries scattered around the chair. My hands were shaking.

'Get up,' Guillaume said and he pulled Pierre to his feet.

'You fucking psycho,' Pierre said to me. 'You could have killed me.'

'I wish I had,' I said.

My trousers were wet from rolling on the damp gravel and I had grit in my mouth. Pierre wiped the blood from his face and stared at it on his hand. He spat on the floor. A thin clot of blood was suspended in the shiny slick of spit.

'I'm losing blood,' he said.

'Shut up,' Guillaume said. 'I'll take you home.'

'My mum's going to kill you for this,' Pierre said. His cheek was red and there was a graze under his eye.

A group of guys from the lycée were watching from the other side of the fence, jeering and shouting. Guillaume pulled at Pierre's arm.

'Let's go before they start.'

They walked away together towards the exit. Pierre turned and shouted:

'Fuck you, fat boy.'

I pulled my chair out from the food; it scraped across the gravel and inside my head. A crow landed on Pierre's burger and started to dig at the meat. I checked my phone. Why hadn't she messaged me?

'Where are you?' I wrote.

But she didn't reply, even though I had risked my arse defending her. Too busy, she'd told me, but not too busy for Stéphane. I got up and hunted among the McDo bags for something to eat. I ate the rest of Guillaume's damp fries. The white potato inside felt like tissue in my mouth.

More and more crows kept landing on the food, four or five of them. They just sit around the jardin all day stuffing their faces on fast food, but they don't get fat. I kicked at the burgers on the ground. I kicked at the crows, at the shreds of pale lettuce, at the paper bags and the mayonnaise and the plastic forks, I kicked until everything turned black, smashed up and dark with earth and gravel.

I couldn't keep it in any more. It kept erupting out of me. I had to tell maman. I had to tell her what I knew. I thought if she knew what I knew then she could help me. She could help me understand what I had seen. She could take her share of the sorrow, because it belonged to her, because I couldn't bear it on my own.

I stood up to walk home. The air was icy and the sky dark, like a bruise. Maybe it would snow. I walked alone through the jardin. I walked past the upright green benches, past the neatly trimmed lawn and the metal hoops of fencing. The gardeners were grappling with a shrub that had blown onto the path, hacking off its branches. Everything in Paris is constrained. Everyone is trying to hold you down, make ordered beauty, afraid that you'll run wild: the guards whistling you off the grass, the gardeners cutting back the trees to bleeding stumps. If you are ugly they will rip you out the way they rip out the flowers as soon as they begin to die. I wanted to be out of this Paris, out of this darkness that was pulling me down.

Teresa was downstairs when I walked into our apartment building. She was stooped over her mop like a vulture waiting for doom. My heart sank. She would want to know why my jacket was ripped, why my jeans were wet. She looked up from cleaning the floor.

'You're home early?' she said. It was a question.

'Yeah, the heating broke down. We got sent home.'

She dipped the mop into the dirty water, pulled it out again, and wrung it out against the bucket sieve.

'It's going to snow.' She pulled her black cardigan around her stout body. 'It'll be minus three tonight.' I said nothing. She was blocking my way.

'Your friend,' she said, 'the girl. She's upstairs.'

I went to get past her. She waited until I was by the lift and then she said:

'Your mother's flight was cancelled.'

I turned back. Her face was sly.

'She came home,' she said.

I ran then. I took the stairs. I took them two at a time. I ran even though my leg was killing me from where I'd fought with Pierre. I ran to try to stop something, but I didn't know what. Around and around, up and up. I held my key out in front of me. I pushed open the apartment door.

Maman was there. I saw her first. She turned to me, her face mangled, her mascara smudged beneath her eyes. Her nose was red and running. Scarlett stood beyond her. She was wearing only a bra and knickers. They were my mother's bra and knickers. Leopard-print and satin, tassels and stuff. Maman bought them after my father left.

Scarlett was swaying in my mother's high heels and boudoir lingerie. She stood beneath the ceiling spotlight. She didn't try to cover herself. She looked at us, her black eyebrows raised, her hand poised below one hip. Her breasts were too small for my mother's bra; her stomach was soft like a peach. Beyond her, in the shadow between two lights, stood Gabriel.

The doom that had been trapped inside me swelled up and burst out, like gas escaping; it spread and rose and filled the corridor, taking up all the space so that it was everywhere, inside me and out, and I could hardly breathe.

'This little slut—' maman said, but Gabriel interrupted.

'There's been a kind of misunderstanding, Paul,' he said.

'Don't give me that crap,' maman said. She shoved at her nose with the back of her hand. 'What do you think I am? She's wearing my fucking underwear.'

'Babe, I can explain.' Gabriel took a timid step towards her. 'We were just taking some photos. This is not what it seems.'

'Not what it seems? I find my thirty-five-year-old boyfriend and the father of my child in my dressing room with a teenage girl wearing my underwear and him taking photos of her on his phone. And you tell me that is not what it seems. Why don't we call the police, then, Gabriel, and ask them what they think? Shall we do that? Shall we see what they say? Let's do that. Why don't we do that right now?'

Saliva fell to the parquet as she spoke.

'Babe, I can explain.'

'How can you explain?' Her voice was madness. 'How can you explain?' She shouted out again. She started to pull at her own clothing, grabbing at her top, then lifting it up high so that her bra and breasts were exposed.

She cried out.

'What about me? Aren't I enough for you?'

Gabriel screwed up his face as if he was afraid to look.

'Babe,' he begged.

And then Scarlett spoke.

'Nothing happened,' she said. 'He just took some photos. That's all.'

Her voice was flat when she said that, weirdly calm. She wasn't afraid of my mother; she wasn't afraid of anyone. She shrugged.

'Nothing happened,' she said again.

And then she turned away and started walking back in the direction of maman's bedroom. Her bony shoulder blades stuck out like wings on her back.

'Where do you think you are going?' maman shouted after her.

Scarlett turned around, her expression insolent.

'Well, I'm not going to walk home like this, am I?'

Maman lunged forward and grabbed Scarlett's left arm.

'You,' she said, 'you're nothing but damaged goods. I knew it from the start.'

'Hey, lady, you should blame your boyfriend, not me,' Scarlett said.

Maman let go of her arm then and grabbed her by the throat.

'How dare you,' she said. 'How dare you come in here and fuck up my life. This is my world. I made it. It's me that controls.'

Her right hand was gripping Scarlett's throat, thumb to one side, fingers on the other, there where there is no flesh, just veins and tendons. Maman's face was screwed up; she had white spittle gathered at the corners of her mouth.

'I decide!' she shouted.

'You're hurting me,' Scarlett cried out. 'Stop.'

'Stop, maman,' I said.

My hand flew up and grabbed maman's hand, wrenched it away from Scarlett's throat. I held it in the air. I saw it tremble and flutter there. She struggled to free herself from my grip.

'Let go of me,' she said.

Scarlett put both her hands to her burning neck. The skin was raw and red where maman had held her.

'You hurt me,' she said. 'You hurt me too much.'

Maman stood breathing hard through her nose, like a horse, her head down. I held on to her wrist. She looked up at me. 'It was never you she wanted,' she said. 'Don't you see that? You were just a way in.'

I don't know what Scarlett did then. I don't remember where she went. I guess she must have gone into my mother's dressing room to get her clothes, because when she came back out into the corridor she was wearing a sky-blue jumper with a pink-and-white unicorn on it. Her face was pale. Her eyes were empty. She looked small and frail inside the fluffy jumper. She didn't look at Gabriel. She didn't speak to him.

I stood in the corner by the front door. I was crying. She came towards me, holding tight to her phone. She stopped in front of me. She was fiddling with the little toys dangling from her phone. I could see the pale freckles on the side of her nose. She had painted thick black sweeps of eyeliner on her eyes. Her neck was still red.

'Why did you do it?' I said.

'I told you, I didn't do anything.'

'Yes, you did. You're here with him. You wore my mother's stuff. You let him take your photo. You told me he was an arsehole.'

She shrugged her shoulders. She was sullen, closed.

'It's no big deal,' she said.

'It is to me,' I said.

'Don't look at me like that. You ought to be pleased. Now you can have your precious maman back.'

She smiled her secret smile and then she leaned forward and kissed me. She kissed me somewhere near my mouth, but not on my mouth. She kissed me so lightly that afterwards, I wondered if she had kissed me at all. When she drew back her head, she was already far away and I knew then she was leaving me.

'Why do you have to destroy everything?' I said. 'Everything around you. You destroy.'

She flinched as if I'd hit her. But still she didn't cry, she didn't blink, she just stared at me, her pupils like tiny bullet holes.

'I can't help the way I am, Paul,' she said.

'Then go,' I said. 'Get out of my life. I don't want you the way you are.'

She stayed a moment longer, not moving, hovering in the doorway while I wept. And then she said, 'It's not true, what she said. You are my friend.'

'Is that what this is? Friendship.'

She shrugged and held her palms up towards me.

And then she opened the door.

'So long, Paul,' she said softly. 'I'll miss you.'

She walked away from me; she left the door wide open after she had gone.

16

I sat with my back against the wall and my head on my knees. My leg was bruised. My body ached. There was silence. Then maman said:

'Why do you do this to me now? Now that I'm old.' Her voice was just a whisper. I didn't know who she was talking to, if she meant Gabriel or me or if it was really my father she was talking to.

Then she clenched her fists and beat at her thighs. 'What have you done to me? You've taken everything you wanted.'

I had nothing to give, nothing I could say.

Gabriel took a step towards her.

'Stay away from me,' she said. 'I want you out. Do you understand?'

'Babe, you don't mean that.'

'You think I don't know?' she said. 'You think I don't know the signs? What, do you think I'm a fool, Gabriel? You think I don't know about men? I know all there fucking is to know about men. I don't want you in Lou's life. You'll never see her again.'

'Come on, babe, you don't mean that, she's my child.'

'Says who?' maman shouted.

He looked confused.

'Well, everyone. Everyone says she is,' he said.

He looked around for help.

'She's got my nose, my eyes.' He laughed; he opened up his hands so they were facing the ceiling. I'd never seen him wrong-footed before. He looked at me, waiting for me to back him up, waiting for me to say, you're right, Gabriel, she looks just like you.

'You think you are the only one? The big daddy?' maman said. She made her mouth go ugly around the word daddy. 'Don't kid yourself, Gabriel.'

He looked at her as if he didn't understand. She stared at him.

'Get out,' she said.

She walked down the corridor and into her bedroom and then she started throwing his clothes out into the corridor. He didn't have that many clothes, a couple of pairs of jeans, some sweatshirts, his leather jacket, his underpants. He didn't need a removal van. She threw his trainers out one by one and they bounded along the corridor and landed near my feet.

It was as if the physical action stoked her anger, because next she ran back along the corridor and into the salon and she grabbed hold of his guitar, the acoustic one, the one he'd played when Scarlett came around. She held it high above her head.

'No, Séverine,' Gabriel said when he saw what she was going to do.

She threw it across the salon and into the corridor. It landed on the parquet and skidded up against the skirting board and fell back. It made a twanging sound as it landed. I heard it crack and splinter. Next she went over to the electric guitar. Gabriel cried out.

'Not the Gibson,' he said. 'Babe, not the Gibson.'

'Yes, the fucking Gibson!' she shouted.

She tried to wrench it off its guitar stand, but it was fixed in, so she kicked at it instead. She kicked it onto the floor and then she kicked at it again, savagely, six times, until the polished auburn wood was ruptured and broken.

'Please, Séverine,' he begged; he stood between the acoustic and the Gibson. 'You've got to stop.'

'Get out,' she shouted.

'I'll go,' he said, 'I'll go. I just need a taxi. Babe, listen to me, just call me a taxi and I'll go.'

Maman stared at Gabriel, and then she laughed out loud, a strange, high-pitched laugh that made me wonder if she was high.

'I'd rather die than call you a taxi.'

That was all she said; no more insults, no more shouting, not another word. She turned away from him and walked into her bedroom, then into her bathroom. She slammed the door and I heard the lock turn.

Gabriel unplugged the Gibson from the amp. He picked it up and turned it over in his hands; he touched it like it was his child. I sat and watched him. After a while, he looked up and saw me there, staring at him.

'Hey, Paul, don't suppose you have a number for a taxi, do you?'

I unlocked my phone and pulled up the number for G7. He came across to me and I passed him the phone.

'Thanks,' he said. He dialled the number and waited for them to pick up. 'You know what, Paul? She'll be fine once she's calmed down a bit. I'll come back and explain. Don't you worry about this. Yeah, hi there, I need a taxi, please.'

After he'd ordered his taxi he went over and started picking up the clothes that were lying in the corridor and stuffing them into a big black leather bag.

The intercom buzzed above my head. I couldn't get up. Gabriel came over to answer it. He stretched across me. The taste of his aftershave hit the back of my mouth. His leg pressed against my leg.

'Excuse me, mate,' he said and then he spoke into the intercom. 'Yeah, I'll be right down.'

He picked up his guitars and the leather bag. He came and stood before me. He looked a little shame-faced then, but only for about a minute, not like he was going to lose any sleep.

'Paul, look, I'm sorry about Scarlett. We were just having a bit of fun, you know, nothing serious. I mean, you guys were never together and we were just taking some pictures for our new album, I'm trying to get some visuals for the band and I think she wanted to send some hot photos to some guy she's after. Maybe when your mum cools down, you could say that to her, that it was nothing, you know, nothing major. Hey, I've got to go, the taxi is downstairs, but tell Lou I'll be back to see her and maybe me and you and Lou, we could hang out, go to Euro Disney one day.' He looked hopeful when he said that; he looked like he honestly believed it could happen.

I shuffled out of his way so that he could get by with his guitars and his bag. He closed the door quietly behind him. I stayed there a while, I don't know how long, and then I got to my feet. My leg had seized up and I couldn't walk properly. I went into maman's bedroom. The bed was made, but the rest of the room was wrecked. There were clothes and high heels and a hairdryer lying on the floor and I wondered if it was maman that had done that or if it was Scarlett. There was no noise from the bathroom. I knocked on the door.

'Maman?' I said.

'Leave me alone,' she said.

'It's not my fault. It was Gabriel that chased her; he wouldn't leave her alone.'

'Go away,' I said. 'I don't want to know.'

I stood there with my face up against the door listening to her cry. I was crying too. It wasn't fair; they made this happen.

The door to her dressing room was open. I went in. The light was on. It was dark outside. The white walls looked grey. There were four full-length mirrors in there. They hung from the front of the cupboards and they were all around me so I could see myself, over and over, for ever.

It was like a shrine to maman; the cashmere, the mousseline blouse, the black leather skirt, all the handbags and belts – everything was waiting for her. She'd said the good thing about my father leaving was that she had more room for her clothes. I ran my hand across her dresses; they swayed a little on their hangers. I stroked the soft suede of her boot; I put my hand inside the opening, reached with my fingers to the tip of the inner sole. I opened her drawers. I looked for the bra. I wondered if Scarlett had taken it with her. But it was there, folded up, put back neatly among the others, harmless now. I pushed my fingers into the cups of satin. I touched the raw edge of the lace. I felt the shape of her.

I stood in front of the mirror and stared at myself, maman's bra hanging by my side, dead and lifeless. Then I grabbed hold of it and I twisted it, the hard metal underwires, one half-moon and then the other. I twisted it until it was broken and deformed. I bent it so that she would never wear it again.

I closed my eyes. I wanted to go to her then, to find her lying on her pink duvet with the curtains open and lamplight on her face. I wanted to take her hand and lead her onto the floor, to lie with her on the white sheepskin rug. I wouldn't try to take her clothes off. I wouldn't call her a slut or push my dick against her. I would lie by her side and softly stroke her hair. I would take away the pain.

I stood by the window in my mother's dressing room with my eyes closed and I felt something fall; my heart, my hope. I don't know what it was. Something dropped suddenly; it fell away inside of me, blunt and final. Down,

down it fell, like a lift plunging inside a dark shaft. I reached out and put my hand against the wall to steady myself. I opened my eyes. But I was still falling.

I walked out of the dressing room; I went into my bedroom. I went to the window. Snow was falling in the dark; huge snowflakes, so large and flat they spun around and around, turning to powder as they hit the ground.

I opened the window. Now there was a gaping hole and the night air was cold against my teeth. Every detail of the courtyard stood out against the snow: two drainpipes ran down beside each other and disappeared into the bottom corner of the wall in a darkened patch. An empty white plastic planter hung from the top balustrade. The snowflakes fell on my face, wet and feathery.

Once I found a bird that had fallen from its nest; it had no feathers, only down. It was a fledgling and it didn't look sad to have died; it looked at peace. It looked happy not to have to go through the pain of living.

I thought about Scarlett and me on the swing. I thought about flying high through the cold air and the thrill of it. It had felt like the beginning of something.

I looked down out of the window. I could see the cobbles in the dark; they shone up at me. The folded shutters of Teresa's apartment glowed white. The girl opposite was sitting at her desk working. The snow wasn't sticking. What else could I do? Stay away from the window, Paul. Cindy will be home soon. Shut the fuck up. I'm not listening to you any more; I've had it with listening to you.

The windows opposite were black, opaque; no amount

of sun would ever light them up. There were metal grates in the stone of the wall. I thought of mouths behind the grates, mouths breathing in and breathing out, calling out to me.

The door opened behind me.

'Paul,' a voice cried out. It was Cindy's voice. 'Paul,' she said again.

I turned around. She was standing against the light of the corridor. She had Lou in her arms. I saw the panic in her face. I tried to remember what the guy on TV said about free-falling; orgasmic, that is what he said. She shifted Lou from her arms up onto her shoulder, and she took two small steps towards me.

'There is too much pain now, Cindy,' I said.

'I know that, Paul.' She looked like she would cry.

'How can you know?' I said. 'You don't know about Scarlett and Gabriel. Maman says it was me that brought her here. I didn't do it, Cindy. I didn't make these things happen. She says it's my fault. It wasn't me, Cindy. You don't know about my father.'

'I know it is not you,' Cindy said, 'that is not who you are.'

'Scarlett has gone,' I said.

She held out her hand to me. Lou's cheek was pushed up against her shoulder; white watery lumps trailed from Lou's mouth across Cindy's sweatshirt. The cold air pressed at my back. Cindy stood just in front of me. She swayed her body from side to side, rocking Lou in her arms.

'You are not your father,' she said.

She said it to me in her strange English, she said it standing there, small and crying, looking at me, holding out her hand. I could smell the fabric conditioner coming off her clothes.

'I'll make you rice, Paul. I'll make you rice like you like.'

I looked at her standing there – she was so small – and I thought about her two kids and how she hadn't seen them for six years and how she'd looked after me all that time and I thought, if I die now, somehow my death will be her death. And I thought how it would be Cindy who would have to clean me up off the cobblestones, the way Essie had to clean my father's sweat off the parquet.

And I thought of Lou left on her own in her cot while Cindy was downstairs hosing me off the courtyard. I thought of Lou and leaving her in all this loneliness. I wasn't my father. Is that what she said?

'I'm going to close the window,' Cindy said, 'so I need you to hold Lou.'

She passed me Lou. Her body was warm and heavy with sleep. I held her in my arms. I had never held her before. Her hands were folded over each other, clasped together as she slept. I touched her hands; they were warm and a little clammy. Her face was shiny. She smelled of milk. The weight of her steadied me, held me in place.

Cindy reached up and shut the windows, then she turned the handle so that the white-painted metal rod rose up and fitted back into its slot and the two windows met in the middle and closed.

The girl opposite was standing at her window, looking at me. Her face was grave, pale, lit up by the light above her. She didn't acknowledge me, she didn't nod, she made no sign, but she was staring straight at me. She saw me there in front of her. I know that.

'Come, Paul,' Cindy said. 'I will make you rice.'

I turned away from the window.

17

I ate without thinking. I used a spoon like I was a baby, shovelling the rice into my mouth, letting myself sink in the warm white grains. Cindy stayed with me; she padded around the kitchen, back and forth between the fridge and the microwave, fixing Lou a bottle. Lou was in her high chair trying to stuff some toy keys into her mouth.

I wondered how Cindy knew what to say to me, how she had the right words. I wondered if it was from reading the Bible that she knew these things, that she had this certainty.

I checked my phone. There was a message waiting from Scarlett.

'You could have trusted me, but you never did. Don't you remember the wounded hearts, Paul? There are some wounds that never heal. Sometimes you die wounded.'

I stared at the message. I read it again.

Lou was banging the keys on the high-chair table, making noises from the back of her throat, trying to get my attention. She had saliva dribbling down her chin.

I stood up.

'I have to go out now, Cindy,' I said.

'Now?' she said, looking at my half-eaten bowl of rice. 'It is so cold outside.'

'Yeah, I know,' I said. 'But I need to go now.'

I texted Scarlett.

'I'm coming,' I wrote.

I went to the front door. I opened it and walked down the stairs, dialling her number as I went, but I couldn't get a signal in the staircase. I started to run down. I checked my phone to see if she had replied. The woman who lives on the second floor was coming up the stairs carrying her shopping. I waited for her to go past me. Teresa was in her lodge. She had the television on loud; I could see the news flickering behind her lace curtains.

I opened the door to our apartment building and I tripped as I stepped over the base of the doorframe. The melting snow made it wet underfoot and I slipped on the pavement. I knocked my ankle against the bins that Teresa had put out. I swore and put out my hand to stop myself falling. I righted myself and I started to run as best I could with my bad leg. I called her on my phone as I ran to her apartment.

I turned onto the Rue d'Assas, past people seeking shelter from the snow under the roof of the bar on the corner. I saw red lights flashing ahead. There was the sound of sirens. People are always getting run over on the Rue d'Assas. One time I saw a guy from our school lying in the middle of the road. He'd got hit by a van when he went to get lunch. But he didn't die.

I ran along the road to where she lived. There were police cars parked up all over the pavement and there was a SAMU ambulance sticking out of the doorway to her apartment building. Red-and-white tape ran from one side of her building to the other; it danced across the bonnet of the ambulance. It trembled in the wind.

A metallic voice on a radio inside the police car said: 'No more cars.'

There were people gathered at the edge of the tape. I stared at the red bonnet of the ambulance and the headlights that lit up our bodies in the dark. It blocked the entrance to the apartment building, so I could not see beyond.

'It's an accident,' the woman beside me said.

'Who is it?' I said to the policewoman standing at the front, the one who was guarding the tape.

'We are responding to an emergency,' she said.

'Is it Scarlett?' I said. 'Is it Scarlett Lacasse?'

I must have shouted that, because she looked at me strangely and she laid her hand on my forearm and I shouted out again. She said something into her radio and the onlookers took a step away from me. A snowflake fell on my cheek; it turned to water with my tears.

'Just tell me,' I said.

Then someone shouted from behind the ambulance, and the policewoman turned from me; she ran along the side of the ambulance into the courtyard. I waited until she had gone and then I ducked under the tape and squeezed myself between the ambulance and the wall on the opposite side.

There were people in the courtyard, people and plants in pots and a parked car covered in white and there were huge crystal snowflakes spinning in the night air. There were emergency workers kneeling on the ground, making a circle, like they were playing some kind of children's game on a blanket of snow. And in the centre of the circle was Scarlett. I went towards her.

My beautiful Scarlett, my friend, she was broken. Her right arm lay flung out behind her. She was wearing her unicorn jumper still, but it was stained and dark with blood. Her skin was greyish-green and transparent, like she had drunk some kind of poison. There was a gape of white between her eyelids. She had a tube coming out of her nose and going into a clear plastic bag, and someone had wrapped a kind of white paper hood around the top of her head. It made me think of Saint Catherine lying in her glass box.

I wanted to touch her. I wanted to tell her I was there.

I stepped towards her. I caught my arm on a tree that was growing in a pot. I pulled myself clear.

One of the emergency workers in the circle looked up and saw me standing there.

'What are you doing?' he said. 'You shouldn't be here.'

'She's my friend,' I said.

I looked down at her face. She looked so cold. I couldn't make her better.

He stood up and came towards me. He had snowflakes caught up in his short grey hair. He called to someone, 'Get this kid out of here.' The ambulance doors were open. I saw the empty stretcher inside. One of the ambulance men pushed past me to get into the driver's seat.

'Stand back,' a voice called out.

. I stepped back. I saw a policewoman holding a woman up by her armpits. I saw a dog spinning on a lead, trying to yank his head out of the collar, trying to break free.

'How about we go somewhere and talk,' a soft voice said to me. It was a policewoman. She wore a hi-vis jacket with reflector bands that flashed silver in the dark. A man called out to her to come over. 'Just give me a minute,' she said. 'You wait here.' She touched my arm. She turned away.

I looked back at Scarlett. They were lifting her body onto a stretcher.

The ambulance was reversing towards her and they were closing the main doors to the courtyard; if I didn't leave now, I would be trapped inside. I would have to tell them what happened. I would have to tell them everything. I didn't want to leave her all alone.

I ran. I slipped between the doors as they were closing. I ducked under the red-and-white tape. A shower of snowflakes fell on me, melting and turning my shoulders wet. I blinked in the dark. I heard a voice cry out in the courtyard behind me. I heard a dog bark. I looked around and hesitated, unsure of what to do. And then I turned and ran back along the Rue d'Assas.

18

They took her away. They gathered her up and took her to where her grandparents lived. She would have hated that, to be buried in the middle of nowhere when all she wanted was Paris. She told me once that her grandparents' village is so dull, even the cows get bored. That is what she said.

I don't know the name of the village where she is buried. But I know what the church looks like. I've seen churches like that in Brittany. They are small, hunched buildings made of dark granite where they hang Christ out in the rain, where they nail him to a blackened cross.

She would never have wanted her funeral there. She would have wanted it at the Chapelle de la Médaille Miraculeuse, where everything shimmers gold and blue, where the angels wrap you in their soft white wings and fly with you to heaven.

César could have saved her if he'd been there, but the housekeeper had taken him out for a walk. The apartment was empty when she got home; she was all alone. Did she know I loved her? Did she drink her vodka and spritz her mouth with her blue and silver breath freshener and climb out onto the balustrade and think of me, the way I think of her, all the time?

I lie in bed and read every message she sent me. I watch each video. I close my eyes and try to remember who she was. I try to imagine the photos she sent to Stéphane, the stuff she must have sent to Gabriel. I try to stop the jealousy that surges still. I keep thinking how, even though she bombarded us with all that information, those images, even though she put her life, her body on our screens, none of us ever really knew Scarlett. I knew her real name, but what else did I know? That she bought her half-bottles of vodka at the corner shop on the other side of the Jardin d'Observatoire, near where we watched the riot that time. I knew that, but I didn't know how to help her.

There were rumours at school. Bad rumours. People saying she'd still been alive in the ambulance, flailing around on the stretcher as they tried to pump her full of blood. Others said she was smashed to pieces, dead all over the courtyard. I said nothing. I gave nothing away.

I try to imagine her in her coffin underground, just sleeping. I wonder if they buried her with her jangly bangles. Did they let her keep her phone? She would have wanted that; all her videos, her pandas from Japan, her photos. What happened to her nipples? I saw them once, beneath a top she wore, pink and hopeful. What happens to your nipples when you die, when they put you in a coffin?

No one from school went to the funeral; the family didn't want anyone to go. Guys from our year hung round outside school instead. Journalists came. They wanted to interview people who knew Scarlett. They didn't stop me as I walked past the gates. I guess I probably didn't look like the kind of guy who would have known her. They took photos of the girls sitting on the pavement crying. They stopped Stéphane and took a photo of him and Inès together; they were holding hands in the photo. Stéphane was wearing that black-and-white scarf with tassels that he thinks makes him look like a tough guy from the hood when we all know his dad is an estate agent in Saint-Germain.

Scarlett. You are lost to me now.

After it happened, maman took me to Megève. She rented a chalet there and we stayed for Christmas. We didn't ski. Maman didn't want to see anyone. She spent the week in her bedroom in the dark talking on the phone to her mother and Estelle. She got up to take me to the doctor; she gave me pills to stop the panic inside my chest that came in waves and made me feel like a butterfly beating my wings against a window to get out.

I took the pills with Coca-Cola in a glass and I lay on a white sofa in the chalet under a silvery fur rug and I watched the Disney Channel. I looked out of the window at the mountains. I watched the figures travelling fast down the slopes. I watched the pink sunlight on the dark pines; I saw the light turn blue, then black. Cindy stayed with me, and Lou. Lou was there too.

I haven't seen Gabriel since maman threw him out that day. Maman won't let him come around and see Lou. For a while I wondered if I should tell the police about Scarlett and him, about the photos they took together. I didn't know what I should say and what I should keep quiet about. I didn't know how to talk about these things that I had seen without bringing them all crashing down on top of me, on top of them. So I said nothing. I keep it all inside my head and it plays there, over and over, a film noir that I cannot stop, even though I try.

Cindy still lives upstairs in her *chambre de bonne*. She's planning on moving to Canada next year, because if she goes to Canada and works there as a nanny, then in five years her children and her husband can come and live with her. They'll get real visas that mean they can stay there for ever. Her kids will be thirteen and fifteen by the time that happens, but Cindy doesn't seem bothered by that. She's doing interviews on Skype in her room upstairs. She showed me photos of one of the families; they look nice. They have two children, a boy and a girl, and in the photo they are standing by a lake laughing. They have big white smiles and wide-open faces. There are tall green trees on the edge of the lake, and the sky is vast and blue behind them.

She hasn't told maman that she is going. She says to me:

'Thank god, Paul, I will find a way back to my children.'

I don't know what maman will do without Cindy. I don't know what I'll do.

Maman still has her business. She travels a lot. She's got a new trainer and he says he's going to make her body even hotter. That's what he says to her when she is doing her sit-ups on the salon floor. 'Ten more makes you a winner, Séverine.'

I see maman looking at her face in the mirror when we get into the lift to go up to our floor. She leans forward and pulls at her eyebrows. She frowns at what she sees. She's planning on getting her breasts done. She discussed it with Estelle last Saturday, when she came round for coffee. Estelle says it's the best remedy she knows of for depression. She gave her the name of her surgeon in Neuilly and she told maman she should go at least three sizes bigger.

'Listen, ma belle, at our age we need every weapon we can get.'

I never told maman about my father, about what I saw. I didn't think she could take any more. But sometimes I look at her face and the sadness there and I get the feeling she knows anyway. It's like she knows, but she's decided not to admit it; she's decided to carry on as if none of it ever happened, as if my dad never did it with men, as if Gabriel never took the photos, as if she never grabbed Scarlett by the throat, as if Scarlett hadn't died. Maybe she figures the greatest risk would be for her to show her wounds.

She's tough, maman. She keeps going. Like my grandmother. She tells everyone that at last she feels free, that she is too lucky to have Lou.

'It's like a rebirth,' she says, 'to be a young mother again. Besides, I have Paul.'

At night she spends a lot of time on the Internet buying handbags and clothes, stuff for Lou and me, cushions for the house, that kind of thing.

My dad did special therapy after the divorce came through in February. He told me it was therapy for sex addiction and that he is over that now, that it was a phase of his life when he was searching for meaning and now he's found it. That's what he told me. He said he was grateful I never told my mother, that it meant that we could start afresh together, wipe the slate clean.

'Thanks to you, Paul, I can salvage my life,' he said.

He's got a new girlfriend. She doesn't know what my dad was doing before she came along. At least, she doesn't act like she knows. She's called Marine and she is like no one I have ever seen him with before. It turns out she's an old girlfriend of his, someone he went out with when he was at school, aged fifteen, when he was about my age. It was my grandmother who got them together again over lunch at their tennis club, when she was worried about my father's depression.

Marine is super-classic, 16ème arrondissement. She used to live in Singapore with her husband, but they got divorced and she came back to Paris with her twin boys, who are a year older than me. They go to my dad's old school in the 16ème. Marine has high cheekbones and she is elegant with no make up. My grandmother says it's a sign of breeding. She wears a gold signet ring on her little finger that has a dark green crest with a tree on it. My grandmother talks to Marine like she is made of glass; she says, 'Of course, Marine, but only if it suits you to come and see us in July?'

In February my grandfather found out he had cancer. They cut it out of him and now he spends his time sitting in his armchair in Neuilly reading *Le Figaro* until he falls asleep. The cancer made him shrink. He looks grateful when we go to see him. 'You've grown, Paul,' he says when I walk into the room. He is grey and tired and when I kiss his cheek, his skin is thin against mine. My father bought him a juicer and they sit together in the sunlight by the window and discuss nutrition and talk about wholegrains as if my grandfather is training for a triathlon.

Next month my father is moving out of his apartment near Le Bon Marché and he and Marine are moving into a big family apartment by the Trocadéro that overlooks the Eiffel Tower. Her sons will live with them too. My father got rid of the Porsche at the beginning of the summer because they couldn't all fit in it. He bought a navy-blue Mercedes estate instead. He drives the boys and Marine to the tennis club in it. That's where they go every weekend, to the tennis club where my grandparents and my aunt and my uncle and my cousins go because Marine's twins play great tennis. They have a ranking that's better than my cousins'.

Every week I go to the Chapelle de la Médaille Miraculeuse and I wait for her to come. I wait with all the others. I hold my medallion in my hand and I rub the hearts to keep them warm. I light a candle in a red glass and watch it flicker there with the others. I say a prayer and then I go and sit on the pew where we sat together that time. I sit and wait. I listen to the hum of the métro vibrating through the chapel and I pray to the Virgin, soft and white, with diamonds that shoot in beams from her sacred hands.

I thought I saw her once. I turned around in my pew and the chapel door was open and I thought I saw her hair against the sunlight, lit up as if she were on fire. I ran to the door and called out her name. I reached out my hand into the long empty courtyard.

I go to school. I take my pills. They block you off and shut you down so you don't feel anything. But the pain is still there. It is a darkness that covers me, like an eclipse of the sun. It bangs up against the sides of me. It is a dead weight hanging from my ankles.

Last week I went to see the orthodontist and he said to me, 'You look in a bad way, Paul.'

I said nothing. He had a metal mirror on a long stick stuck in the back of my mouth at the time, so it was difficult to reply.

'I went through a tough patch when I was young,' he said. He was wearing special wrap-around yellow protector glasses and I could see his eyes close up, staring down at me, sorrowful brown eyes floating above mine.

'You learn to live with it. That is what happens, Paul. You keep going. You work hard. The scar hardens over.' He was fiddling with my brace and a piece of gunk flew off through the air. 'You become an orthodontist.' He laughed when he said that, but his face was sad still.

Sometimes on the weekends I go with Lou to the Jardin du Luxembourg. Mostly Cindy comes with us, but not today because she is picking up maman's dry-cleaning. I push Lou along the Rue d'Assas in her pushchair; she can walk now, but she doesn't like walking far.

When we get into the jardin I show her the beehives and I tell her how the bees go into their houses to make honey. We cross the tarmac dalle where I used to hang out when I was little. The sun is out and the mothers are sunbathing. The guys have taken off their shirts to play basketball and the mothers sit and watch their naked black chests through half-closed eyes.

I push her across to the ponies and we stand in the queue and wait. I pay the pony man with the staring eye, but I won't let him kiss Lou as he puts her in the little green carriage. I walk along beside the carriage and the ponies walk ahead. The earth smells of horse piss and all the hedgerows are green. We turn around by the trees and come back to the benches where the parents wait. I reach in and take Lou out of the carriage.

After the ponies, Lou sits back down in her buggy and she says Spider-Man or she says a word as near to Spider-Man as she can get. She is pointing to the playground. It is called Le Poussin Vert, but Lou and I call it the Spider-Man Park. It has climbing frames and roundabouts, zip wires and trains to play on.

'OK, Lou, we'll go.'

I pay the man at the ticket box and he stamps my hand with a picture of a little chick and he stamps Lou's plump hand and we pass through the metal turnstile and I buy a Coca-Cola lollipop for Lou and a strawberry one for me.

We go and sit in the sandpit. That's what Lou likes best, sitting in the sandpit and filling up a plastic bucket with sand or chewing on her red plastic starfish. Sometimes we go on the roundabout, but sometimes that's too scary. Today we just sit in the sand. I clean her nose for her and she says: 'Gâteau, gâteau.'

'OK, Lou, but this is your last one.' I hand her the vanilla Prince Lu she loves. I make little crescent-shaped piles of sand and I tell her they are croissants. Every time I finish a croissant, Lou bashes it down with her plastic spade.

Maman calls me on her mobile.

'Where are you?' she says.

'At the jardin.'

'Have you got Lou with you?'

'Yeah,' I say, 'I've got Lou.'

'Are you coming home for lunch?'

I don't reply straightaway. I am watching Lou as she slaps at the mounds around her, her mouth pursed in concentration, her eyelashes long and dark against her cheek.

'I got you the Venetian pizza you like, Paul,' maman says, her voice is silken. 'With spicy oil.'

I stand up and brush the sand off my legs. I know what she wants.

'I'll come,' I say.

Then I turn to Lou.

'Come on, bébé, it's time to go. Maman needs us.'

Lou looks up at me and smiles. She has teeth now.

She points a stubby finger.

'Gâteau?' she says and she holds one finger up in front of her eye. 'Gâteau?' she says again, trying to wheedle one more out of me before we head home.

I bend down and kiss her soft hair. She smells of vanilla and wet sand. I hold out my hand and she grips it in hers. Her hand is damp and sandy in mine. She holds on to my fingers and uses me to stand up, balancing herself against my leg.

'Come on, Lou,' I say. 'Let's go home.'

We walk back along the path near where I first saw Scarlett and Stéphane kissing. The little flowers are out like they were that day. They are different than all the other flowers in the jardin; they are not here for show in grand flowerbeds or planted in big stone vases. They grow up all on their own; they push their way through the dark earth and the dead leaves, and their beauty makes me sad.

I asked a gardener once what they were. He said they're miniature cyclamen. He said they represent true love.

They are a pale violet colour and their petals are thin and unfolding, almost transparent. I bend down and pick one; they have a liquid running through their stems that keeps them standing upright.

The breeze blows through the cyclamen and all the little heads nod and flutter and I think of you, Scarlett. I miss you.

I miss you too much.

Acknowledgements

Thank you to Harriet Moore, my agent, who understood Paul from the very beginning and who helped me throughout. I am extremely grateful to my editors Judy Clain and to Paul Baggaley for their wisdom and editorial direction. I would like to thank Tracey Roe, Pamela Marshall, Alexandra Hoopes at Little Brown and Kish Widyaratna and Nicholas Blake at Picador.

I would like to express my great thanks to Claudia Shear, Lily Reece and Laure de Gramont who so generously shared their knowledge, judgement and insight. I thank Tim Pears for giving me both precious advice and the confidence to go back to my original voice.

Many people helped me in significant ways; thank you to Tom Alden, Alexis André, Alice Armstrong-Scales, Vincent Aslangul, Louise Bartlett, Renaud de Beaugourdon, Nick Birts, Stéphane Brossard, Penny Budgen, Hannah Burbidge, Jean-Pascal and Charlotte Bus, Laurent Buttazzoni, Karen Charlett, Xavier Chaumette, Sarah Cherqui-Fürst, Lucy Cornell, Henrietta Courtauld, Marie-Laure Dauchez, Jane Darling, Marie Donnelly, Sarah Drake, Christian Dumais-Lvowski, Rosalina Enriquez, Laurent Faury, Joséfa Fernandes, Robert Ferrell, Amanda Foreman, Natasha

Acknowledgements

...soni, Hélène Harvey, Jodie Hutchins, Tran ...a, Isabelle Jordan-Ghizzo, Felicity Gillespie, Lizzy ..., Molly Laub, Christian Louboutin, Lulu Lytle, ...Maxted, Marcus Reuben, Catherine Roggero, Marie-...l Roux, Sam Rudd, Fleur Scott, Beverley Thompson, Charlotte Thompson, Sarah Turnbull, Wendy Washbourn, Rozelle Webster, Edyta Styga and Dorota Woloszyn. Thank you to my parents George and Charlotte Drake.

All my love and thanks I give to Rupert, Lily, Hathorn, Peony, Sapphire and Gisèle. You inspire me with your love and boundless support.